FROM THE NANCY DREW FILES

THE CASE: Nancy seeks to protect a track star who is running a dangerous race against sabotage.

CONTACT: Samantha Matero's father has come to Carson Drew for help, and Carson enlists Nancy to the cause.

SUSPECTS: Daniel Abrams—*The former track coach at Brookline. Samantha's father cost him his job, and now Samantha may pay the price.*

Lina Coleman—*Her heated rivalry with Samantha for the top spot on the track team may have taken a sinister new spin.*

Matthew Lee—*Samantha's former boyfriend has taken up with the enemy, Lina, and he may want to prove he's on the winning side.*

COMPLICATIONS: Nancy's doing everything she can to keep Samantha safe. But with Paul Johnson around, it may be her relationship with Ned that's in real danger.

Books in The Nancy Drew Files™ Series

#1 SECRETS CAN KILL
#2 DEADLY INTENT
#3 MURDER ON ICE
#4 SMILE AND SAY MURDER
#5 HIT AND RUN HOLIDAY
#6 WHITE WATER TERROR
#7 DEADLY DOUBLES
#8 TWO POINTS TO MURDER
#9 FALSE MOVES
#10 BURIED SECRETS
#11 HEART OF DANGER
#16 NEVER SAY DIE
#17 STAY TUNED FOR DANGER
#19 SISTERS IN CRIME
#31 TROUBLE IN TAHITI
#35 BAD MEDICINE
#36 OVER THE EDGE
#37 LAST DANCE
#41 SOMETHING TO HIDE
#43 FALSE IMPRESSIONS
#45 OUT OF BOUNDS
#46 WIN, PLACE OR DIE
#49 PORTRAIT IN CRIME
#50 DEEP SECRETS
#51 A MODEL CRIME
#53 TRAIL OF LIES
#54 COLD AS ICE
#55 DON'T LOOK TWICE
#56 MAKE NO MISTAKE
#57 INTO THIN AIR
#58 HOT PURSUIT
#59 HIGH RISK
#60 POISON PEN
#61 SWEET REVENGE
#62 EASY MARKS
#63 MIXED SIGNALS
#64 THE WRONG TRACK
#65 FINAL NOTES
#66 TALL, DARK AND DEADLY
#68 CROSSCURRENTS
#70 CUTTING EDGE
#71 HOT TRACKS
#72 SWISS SECRETS
#73 RENDEZVOUS IN ROME
#74 GREEK ODYSSEY
#75 A TALENT FOR MURDER
#76 THE PERFECT PLOT
#77 DANGER ON PARADE
#78 UPDATE ON CRIME
#79 NO LAUGHING MATTER
#80 POWER OF SUGGESTION
#81 MAKING WAVES
#82 DANGEROUS RELATIONS
#83 DIAMOND DECEIT
#84 CHOOSING SIDES
#85 SEA OF SUSPICION
#86 LET'S TALK TERROR
#87 MOVING TARGET
#88 FALSE PRETENSES
#89 DESIGNS IN CRIME
#90 STAGE FRIGHT
#91 IF LOOKS COULD KILL
#92 MY DEADLY VALENTINE
#93 HOTLINE TO DANGER
#94 ILLUSIONS OF EVIL
#95 AN INSTINCT FOR TROUBLE
#96 THE RUNAWAY BRIDE
#97 SQUEEZE PLAY
#98 ISLAND OF SECRETS
#99 THE CHEATING HEART
#100 DANCE TILL YOU DIE
#101 THE PICTURE OF GUILT
#102 COUNTERFEIT CHRISTMAS
#103 HEART OF ICE
#104 KISS AND TELL
#105 STOLEN AFFECTIONS
#106 FLYING TOO HIGH
#107 ANYTHING FOR LOVE
#108 CAPTIVE HEART
#109 LOVE NOTES
#110 HIDDEN MEANINGS
#111 THE STOLEN KISS
#112 FOR LOVE OR MONEY
#113 WICKED WAYS
#114 REHEARSING FOR ROMANCE
#115 RUNNING INTO TROUBLE

The Nancy Drew Files™ 115

RUNNING INTO TROUBLE

CAROLYN KEENE

AN ARCHWAY PAPERBACK
Published by POCKET BOOKS
New York London Toronto Sydney Tokyo Singapore

AN ARCHWAY PAPERBACK *Original*

An Archway Paperback published by
POCKET BOOKS, a division of Simon & Schuster Inc.
1230 Avenue of the Americas, New York, NY 10020

Produced by Mega-Books, Inc.

ISBN: 0-671-50358-8

First Archway Paperback printing June 1996

10 9 8 7 6 5 4 3 2 1

Printed in the U.S.A.

IL 6+

Chapter One

"I feel like I just ran a marathon!" Nancy Drew exclaimed as she steered her blue Mustang into the driveway.

"Only without leaving the gym," George Fayne replied, groaning as she swung her long legs out of the sporty car. "That aerobics class is a killer. I'm not sure I can take another step."

"Not even for food?" Nancy teased.

"Well," George said, "I just *might* have enough energy to crawl to a refrigerator."

Nancy grinned as she unlocked the Drews' front door and led the way toward the kitchen. Despite George's complaints, Nancy knew her tall, slim friend had plenty of energy. George was definitely in great shape.

"So what's for lunch?" George asked, perching

on a stool at the kitchen bar and running a hand through her short dark hair.

Nancy opened the refrigerator and peered inside. "Let's see, we have salami, cold chicken, cheese, potato salad, or that good old standby, peanut butter and jelly."

"I'll take it," George joked, reaching for a loaf of bread. As she spoke, the phone on the counter rang.

"Drew residence." Nancy smiled when she recognized the familiar voice. "Oh, hi Dad! We just got back. . . . Yes, George is here." She paused. "Yes, she's still into running. . . . Right now?" Nancy's tone became serious. "We're on our way, Dad."

Nancy hung up the receiver and reached for her bag.

Her father, Carson Drew, was a respected lawyer in the town of River Heights. At times he called on his daughter for assistance with a case, and Nancy was always happy to help out. "Dad's got a job for us," she said, tossing George her jacket. "Let's go."

"Without lunch?" George asked in a weak voice, looking wistfully at the sandwich fixings.

Nancy laughed. "Cut off some cheese for each of us. I'll grab some bread, and we'll eat on the way."

A few minutes later they were weaving through afternoon traffic on their way to Carson Drew's office.

"Why did your dad ask if I was still running?" George asked, tucking the last of her makeshift sandwich into her mouth.

Nancy flipped her long reddish blond hair over her shoulder and glanced at her friend. "He has a colleague—Carlos Matero from Brookline—in his office. Matero's daughter is on the Brookline High School cross-country team. Apparently she was injured while training. Her father seems to believe that it wasn't an accident. Dad thinks your input as a runner will be helpful."

"Matero . . . I think there was an article about her in the paper," George said. "Her name is Sandra . . . or Stephanie . . . no, it's Samantha. Samantha Matero. She's supposed to be an incredible runner—even scholarship material."

"Well, her father is thinking of slapping a lawsuit on the Brookline athletic department," Nancy said, turning into a parking space. "I get the idea that Dad is trying to talk him out of it."

A few minutes later they were ushered into Carson Drew's comfortable office, where Nancy was greeted with a hug and George with a big smile.

"Thanks for coming," Mr. Drew said, his eyes crinkling up at the corners as he grinned. The gray streaks at his temples just made him more handsome, Nancy thought as she planted a kiss on his cheek.

A short stocky man with a ruddy face and

silver hair rose from his chair to greet the two girls as Mr. Drew made the introductions.

Nancy eyed Mr. Matero with interest. His well-cut suit was expensive, and the gold clip on his tie matched the heavy cuff links in his sleeves. He was older than she had expected—older than most men who had teenage daughters—and she wondered if Samantha was the youngest of the family.

"Please sit down," Carson said, indicating the chairs by the coffee table. He turned to Mr. Matero. "Carlos, why don't you tell Nancy and George what happened to Samantha."

Mr. Matero nodded and leaned forward in his chair. "Samantha is our . . . my only child," he began. "My wife was killed in an automobile accident two years ago, so I became both mother and father to Samantha." He cleared his throat. "But I don't think I'm being overprotective," he said defensively. "There were a couple of accidents before Samantha's—minor accidents, but accidents, nonetheless. There's something wrong in the athletic department of that school, and I intend to get to the bottom of it. Samantha's being sabotaged!"

"Can you tell us more about the accident?" Nancy prompted.

"Samantha was training the day after a heavy rain. She went down in a hole on the course and sprained her ankle. It was a nasty sprain. Daniel

Abrams—he's the Brookline athletic director, or *was*—said the hole was a washout from the rain, but Samantha disagreed. She said it looked as if the hole had been dug and covered with brush."

Nancy glanced over at George, who had had a lot of experience running on weather-damaged tracks.

"A heavy rain can cause a bad washout," George said.

"It was not the weather!" Mr. Matero replied sharply, his ruddy complexion flushing even more. "It was not even negligence. It was deliberate!"

Nancy nodded sympathetically. "But," she said, "wouldn't it be difficult to put one particular runner in harm's way? Doesn't the team run together as a group over the cross-country course?"

"Yes, but my daughter is almost always the lead runner, so she would be the first to encounter any danger such as the hole," Mr. Matero argued. "The only other person on the team who might have reached it first was Lina Coleman. And it's quite possible she may have set it up herself. There's a big rivalry between them, and Samantha usually beats Lina in races."

"I've read about your daughter's running ability," George said. "She's awesome."

Mr. Matero warmed to the compliment. "She is," he said proudly. "She's broken some school records. And her goal is to earn a cross-country scholarship. But it appears that someone doesn't want her to reach that goal."

Mr. Matero took a deep breath. "And now Samantha's getting these threatening phone calls at home."

"Phone calls?" Nancy repeated.

Mr. Matero nodded. "You see, after the accident I lobbied some friends of mine on the school board to take action."

"Did they?" George asked.

"Yes. Finally they recommended that Daniel Abrams, the head coach, be suspended from the athletic department until this matter is cleared up. He's teaching only academic subjects now."

"On what grounds was he suspended?" Nancy asked.

"On the grounds that he was pushing his runners too hard. That he took risks with their safety. And also that he couldn't control his athletes. Many of the kids at school aren't happy about Abrams's suspension, and I'm sure the phone calls to my daughter are coming from one of these kids. But I can't prove it."

"Do you think it's Lina Coleman?"

Mr. Matero shrugged. "Hard to tell. A lot of Brookline's athletes are furious with Samantha because I took action against the coach. They think she put me up to it. Abrams was a popular coach." He paused, then sighed heavily. "The board action backfired. Now even Samantha is mad at me because the District Athletic Association—backing up the school board—is now threatening to disqualify the Brookline team from competition. The association thinks the athletic program could be endangering students' welfare. If Samantha doesn't compete, it would wipe out her chance for a scholarship, and everyone else's. I wish I'd just gone ahead and filed a lawsuit."

Carson Drew leaned toward Nancy. "I've suggested to Carlos that you and George enroll at Brookline as transfer students and do an inside investigation. Maybe we can get to the bottom of this without dragging it through the courts."

"Maybe," Mr. Matero said. He didn't sound convinced. "Now that Samantha's ankle has almost healed, she wants to go back on the team. But I'm very nervous about letting that happen until I find out who sabotaged the course, and why. One more injury could put a permanent end to her running career. She's in danger, and I need your help, Ms. Drew."

Nancy stared out the wide window of the office and pondered the situation. Was this a case of an overprotective parent—or was something really going on at Brookline? What if Samantha's "accident" *had* been planned, maybe by a jealous competitor? And who was making the phone calls? The ousted coach? Angry students?

Mr. Matero shifted impatiently in his chair, then said anxiously, "I thought you and Ms. Fayne could get on the cross-country team and get a firsthand look."

"George wouldn't have any trouble making the team," Nancy said. "But I don't have her experience in running."

"No, Nan, but you're in good shape," George pointed out. "You could probably get on the team."

Nancy turned to Mr. Matero. "Who would know why we were really at the school?"

"The principal, Mr. Lombardi. I've already called him to discuss the situation. He'll see that you're introduced as senior transfer students. The accidents reflect poorly on his administrative record, and he'd like to get the board off his back."

"Understandable," Nancy murmured. "And Samantha? Would she know?"

Mr. Matero nodded. "Yes, we've discussed it. She knew I was coming to talk to Carson today. And she knew that the options were either a lawsuit or an undercover investigation. She's not much in favor of either," he added, "even though she'd like it cleared up. She's getting a lot of peer pressure about Abrams."

"Tell me about the phone calls," Nancy said. "Is the voice a man's or a woman's? And what does the caller say?"

Mr. Matero reached up and nervously pulled

at his tie. "You can't tell if it's a man or a woman," he replied. "It's a voice that's been electronically distorted, as though the message has been taped and then is played back at the wrong speed. I picked up the extension one night and listened."

"And the message?" Nancy asked.

"Always the same," Mr. Matero replied. "'Call off your father or else.'"

The buzzer on Mr. Drew's phone sounded, and he reached over and picked up the receiver. After listening for a moment, he said, "Yes, of course. Send her in." He swiveled in his chair to face the others. "Samantha's here," he said quietly. "Apparently she's received another threat."

Mr. Matero rose out of his chair as the door to the inner office burst open and a tall slender girl with short, dark hair entered the room on crutches.

"I can't take it anymore," she announced, her brown eyes flashing with anger. A piece of white paper was clutched in her hand as she awkwardly lowered herself into a chair. "I just can't take it!"

Mr. Matero hastily made the introductions. "What happened, Samantha?"

"I went out to my car after last period, and this was jammed under my windshield wiper. And whoever did it broke the wipers on both sides."

Mr. Matero squeezed his daughter's hand and said, "This has gone too far. Who would do such a thing?"

Samantha just shook her head, too upset to reply. She pushed her hair out of her face and wiped a tear from her eye.

"May I see the note?" Nancy asked, reaching for the piece of paper. She unfolded it and read it silently. When she saw what it said, she drew a quick breath. Turning to Samantha, she said, "I'd be upset, too."

Written crudely with a black felt pen, the message said: "This time your ankle, next time your neck."

Chapter Two

ON MONDAY MORNING traffic into Brookline from River Heights was heavy. Though the school was only twenty miles from Nancy's home, the ride had taken well over a half hour. Stopped outside the high school at yet another red light, Nancy glanced worriedly at the clock on the dash.

"I'm going to drop you at the entrance," she said to George. "You go in while I park, and let Mr. Lombardi know we're here. I'll meet you in his office."

"Sounds like a plan," George replied, reaching over the seat for her backpack. "See you inside." She shut the car door and disappeared into the throng of students on the front steps of Brookline High, while Nancy turned into the crowded parking lot adjacent to the school. In front of her, a shiny black Jeep Cherokee, with flashy red and gold detailing, navigated the long row of parked vehicles and then veered into an empty slot near the end. Nancy slipped the Mustang into the space beside it.

She glanced in the mirror to check her hair and apply some lip gloss before reaching for the door handle. But to her surprise the door seemed to open on its own.

"You look perfect to me," a husky voice declared.

Startled, Nancy looked up into a pair of mischievous chocolate brown eyes fringed with dark lashes. The driver of the Cherokee extended his hand to help her out of the car.

Nancy grinned. "Are you the official welcoming committee?" she asked, swinging out of her seat.

"Only for selected students, and believe me, you have been selected!" the guy replied, still holding her hand. "I was watching you in the rearview mirror as I was driving. And I said to myself, 'Paul, this is definitely a time to be friendly.'" He laughed, revealing a set of perfect white teeth. "I'm Paul Johnson."

Drop-dead handsome, Nancy thought, taking in the unruly mop of light brown curls that licked at the collar of his short-sleeved knit shirt. And buffed, too, with biceps straining at the cuffs.

"And you're . . ." He tilted his head to one side and looked curiously at her.

"I'm Nancy Drew," she replied with a smile. "I'm a transfer student. This is my first day at Brookline." She looked at her watch. "And I'm late. I have to pick up my class schedule from Mr. Lombardi."

"I'll walk you to the office," Paul said, taking her elbow. A pleasant shiver went up Nancy's arm at his touch. "I saw that you dropped someone off," Paul continued.

Nancy nodded. "You *have* been watching me!" she exclaimed. "That was my friend George Fayne. She's transferring, too."

Paul guided her up the wide steps in front of the school and into the building, casually greeting friends as they passed. "Here's Lombardi's office," he said. "I'll see you later, Nancy Drew." His eyes crinkled in a smile as he opened the door for her. "Yes, I definitely will," he said softly.

Nancy watched as his broad shoulders disappeared into a crowd of students in the hall. Maybe this case would be more fun than she'd thought.

Inside the office, George and Mr. Lombardi were waiting.

"Your reason for being here is strictly confidential," the principal assured them, waving aside Nancy's apologies for being late. "Even my secretary doesn't know why you're here. I've arranged for you to have light class loads to give you time to investigate, but there's one thing I'm afraid I can't fix without arousing suspicion." He sighed and shook his head. "There's no way I can demand that you be put on the cross-country team. You'll have to try out and take your chances with the rest of the students."

"Right," Nancy said. "We're prepared to do that." Even though her tone was confident, she still had some doubt about her ability to make the team. She and George had run more than their usual distance over the weekend, and George had assured her that she was good team material. However, Nancy wondered if she was hearing an honest appraisal—or the loyal voice of an old friend. She would be glad when the tryouts were over.

Mr. Lombardi handed each of them a sheet of paper. "Here are your homeroom assignments and your class schedules. If you can solve this case, you'll be taking a big problem off my hands." He gave them a small smile. "Good luck, ladies."

Back out in the hall, surrounded by milling students, Nancy and George compared schedules.

"This is good. I've got Sheila Keenan for history," Nancy said, "Samantha said she had her for history, too. Keenan's the assistant coach who took over when Abrams was suspended."

She looked at George's schedule. "Do we have any classes together?"

"Doesn't look like it," George replied, studying her schedule. "Oh, no! I'm taking physics—ugh! But we do have a free period together in the afternoon. And Mr. Lombardi said we should report to the gym for cross-country tryouts at four today."

"Don't remind me," Nancy groaned.

"Don't sweat it! You'll do fine," George said. Then she asked, with a glint in her eye, "Who was the hunk at the office door with you?"

"I'll tell you about him at lunch," Nancy said as the warning bell rang.

"I can't stand the suspense," George joked as she waved goodbye to Nancy.

The girls moved in opposite directions, carried along by the flow of students. Nancy's first period was history. She followed two girls into the class and chose a seat toward the back so she could easily observe the other students. Samantha came in by herself and took an aisle seat by the door that allowed ample room for her crutches.

Nancy watched as Samantha pulled out a book and trained her attention on the pages, as if to block out the conversation of two students in the next row. When Nancy heard the boy call the girl Lina, she studied her closely. The girl fit the description Samantha had given her of Lina Coleman, her arch rival on the team. The white blond hair, pulled into a single braid, was a contrast to her heavily made-up eyes and bright red lips. Dressed in a sleek black jumpsuit that showed off her perfect figure, Lina oozed confidence as she laughed and chatted loudly with the guy next to her.

Nancy's observations were interrupted by the arrival of Sheila Keenan, who came briskly into the room and closed the door firmly behind her, only to have it immediately opened by Paul Johnson. Casually he sauntered in and skimmed the class with his eyes. He waved to Nancy and gave her a big grin before lowering his muscular frame into a desk near the front.

Nancy smiled, grateful for his welcome in this room full of strangers. Thoughts of her boyfriend, Ned Nickerson, surfaced in her mind, and Nancy pushed them aside with a twinge of guilt. She felt a little uneasy. Why? she wondered. Because she felt so attracted to Paul Johnson? That was silly! He had only walked her in from the car and waved at her in the classroom. But he *was* cute.

The greeting wasn't lost on Ms. Keenan, who looked pointedly at her watch and then at Paul.

As the period progressed, Nancy got the impression that Sheila Keenan didn't miss much. The attractive teacher had complete control of her class and seemed confident of her ability. Dressed in slim pants and a chic blazer that hugged her trim figure, Ms. Keenan appeared to be only a few years older than most of her students and had a good rapport with them.

When the period ended, Nancy approached her and introduced herself.

"Mr. Lombardi tells me that you and another River Heights transfer student are interested in trying out for cross-country," Ms. Keenan said, after giving her a warm welcome. She interrupted herself to motion to Samantha, who was just leaving the room. "Samantha, come and meet Nancy Drew. She's a runner."

"Hi, Nancy," Samantha said, acting as if she had never seen her before. "Glad to meet you."

Nancy grinned. "I'm glad to meet you, too." Perfect, she thought. No one would guess they'd ever met.

"To be fair," Ms. Keenan continued, "before you go through tryouts, Nancy, I need to tell you that Brookline may be disqualified from district competition. We've had some unfortunate accidents from overzealous coaching. All very minor until"—she put a sympathetic arm around Samantha's shoulders—"until Samantha's accident. I'm sure you've heard of Samantha's fine reputation as a runner."

Nancy nodded. "I have."

"Naturally, we hope the disqualification won't happen, but the district is still undecided." The period bell rang, cutting short any further explanation. "See you this afternoon, girls."

On her crutches, Samantha moved toward the

door, and Nancy followed. "I have a free period. I'll walk you to your next class," Nancy said to Samantha. Then, in a hushed voice, she asked, "What did Ms. Keenan mean about overzealous coaching?"

"Keenan thinks Abrams put too much emphasis on winning, that he worked the team too hard," Samantha explained. "She thinks that if he hadn't had us run the day after the rain, I wouldn't have messed up my ankle." Samantha stopped at a classroom door. "Who knows? He *was* awfully tough on me and my extracurricular activities."

"What do you mean?" Nancy asked.

"I don't want to talk about it." Samantha's voice was suddenly sharp. "It's nothing." Then she hesitated. "Sorry, I didn't mean to snap. Look, if you and George want to check out the course to get a feel for it before tryouts, I'll have a little time later this afternoon."

"Great! But can you walk that far on crutches?"

"Sure. The ankle is practically healed. The crutches are just to help me get from class to class. My dad made me bring them today," she added, rolling her eyes. "I walk around without them at home, and I've even done some in-place jogging on my home equipment." She opened the classroom door. "I'll meet you outside the gym at three-fifteen."

* * *

The sky was overcast when Samantha led Nancy and George out to the cross-country course, which had its beginning and ending at the edge of the school's playing field, looping through woods and fields in between. Samantha, surprisingly mobile on her crutches, kept up a walking pace with Nancy and George as she pointed out various landmarks.

"Pitfall Pond," she explained with a smile as they circled a small body of water. "This is where I fell," she continued, pointing at a wooded spot on the narrow trail. She raked at some leaves on the ground with one of her crutches. "The hole's filled in by now." She shook her head. "You'd think I would have seen it. Really, it was the strangest thing—almost like something reached out and grabbed my ankle."

"This is a pretty challenging course," Nancy said, looking back at the ground they'd covered.

Samantha nodded. "Yeah, it goes over some tough terrain. You haven't lived until you've hit Mount Fuji on a hot and humid afternoon." She pointed ahead to a steep hill. "I don't know who named it, but everybody dreads it." She sighed wistfully. "I never thought I'd see the day when I'd actually look forward to running up Fuji."

"When will the doctor let you start running again?" George asked.

"I see her after school tomorrow, and she's practically promised me that I'll turn in the crutches. I've just *got* to run in the big prelim next week. There'll be two other schools competing and I have to make a showing."

"After three weeks on crutches, will you be ready?" Nancy asked.

Samantha shrugged. "I hope so. I've been doing upper-body workouts since the accident—arm curls and bench presses—and breathing exercises. Also stationary cycling and jogging. And I'll have a week to get my legs back in shape."

"That's what I call determination," George said as they came back in view of the school.

"You've got that right!" Samantha exclaimed. "Lina Coleman is not going to ruin my chances for a scholarship."

"Speaking of Lina . . ." Nancy said. She nodded her head toward a bank of bleachers, where Lina was standing beside Sheila Keenan.

"I'm surprised she's not in the weight room," Samantha said. "That's where I'm headed. I hope she's not there when I get there, because I don't want to get anywhere near her!" The sharp edge in her voice diminished. "Hey, good luck with tryouts, you two."

The tryouts, which consisted of several sprints plus an endurance run, went quickly. Both boys and girls were trying out, and Nancy and George were among the first to finish.

"You were great!" George said to Nancy as they came off the trail and jogged toward Ms.

Keenan. "You don't have to worry about getting on."

"Thanks," Nancy replied. "We'll see. It's a cinch that *you're* on."

Sheila Keenan smiled as they approached. "Nice job," she said, looking at George. "You've obviously had a lot of experience. In fact, you both have good times. I'll post a roster tomorrow. It looks as though we're going to have the best team in the district."

Still smiling, Coach Keenan turned to speak to some of the other students, and Nancy and George headed for the locker room. As they changed, Nancy couldn't help remarking, "Keenan's certainly got a positive attitude. You'd never guess that the team might be pulled from competition."

George opened her mouth to reply, but an acid voice from behind cut her off.

"What do you expect her to do? Roll over and play dead because of one spoiled brat?"

Nancy turned to face Lina Coleman.

"Your friend Samantha managed to get Coach Abrams suspended," Lina said. "But she's not going to ruin *everyone's* chances to compete with her playacting. Especially not mine."

Nancy studied Lina for a moment and then said, "I'm not sure I know what you mean. My friend and I are new at Brookline, and we just met Samantha Matero."

"Well, let me warn you about her, then," Lina continued. "She'll do anything to get her own way. Samantha wasn't injured. She staged her little accident to get even with Coach Abrams. She's faking it!"

Chapter Three

"GET EVEN with Coach Abrams?" Nancy repeated, puzzled. "Why?"

Lina's mouth curled into a sneer. "Because he put Samantha on probation for breaking training rules. She showed up late for almost every practice, if she showed at all. So he threatened to kick her off the team."

"Why would she jeopardize her own chances for a scholarship?" George asked. "That doesn't make sense."

"She's not jeopardizing anything! She'll make a miraculous recovery just before the big race. But she got the result she wanted with her so-called injury. The best coach this school ever had was bumped out of the athletic department."

Lina turned and strode out of the locker room, leaving Nancy and George staring at each other.

"Wow," George said. "I wonder if Samantha *is* faking it. She was pretty quick on those crutches out on the course today."

"I was thinking the same thing," Nancy mused as she and George left the locker room and started down the hall. "And I wonder why Samantha was breaking training if the scholarship was so important to her. You know, she said something to me earlier about Coach Abrams interfering with her extracurricular activities, but she wouldn't explain. I'd give anything to know what she meant. . . ."

"Maybe I can help."

Nancy whirled around and looked up into Paul Johnson's laughing eyes.

"Paul!" she said. "Where did you come from?"

"The gym and points west," he said.

Nancy introduced George, and Paul flashed her a smile before turning back to Nancy. "Are you still willing to give *anything* to find out about Samantha Matero's extracurricular activities?" Paul teased.

"I'm curious, but it's not that important," Nancy said, trying to sound casual. She didn't want to appear too interested or someone might suspect she was investigating. "Why do you ask?" she said.

"How about a date tomorrow afternoon over at Java Village in return for immediate information about Samantha Matero?" Paul looked expectantly at Nancy.

Nancy didn't have to think about Paul's offer for long. "It's a deal," she said.

"Excellent!" Paul said, laughing as they made their way toward the main entrance. "The barter system is alive and well. Come with me," he added in a stage whisper. "Uncle Paul is going to tell you the strange but true tale of the Samantha-Matthew-Lina triangle."

"Is that something like the Bermuda Triangle?" George quipped.

"Similar but more dangerous." Paul led them outside, where they sat on the broad steps in front of the school. In contrast to the bustling morning throng, only a few students passed them, and Nancy noticed that the parking lot, off to the left, was almost empty.

"Okay," Nancy said, a little unsettled by Paul's nearness. Their knees touched and she noticed the citrus scent of Paul's aftershave drifting toward her. She pulled her mind back to the case and asked, "Who's Matthew?"

"Matthew Lee . . . honor student, star basketball player, recent boyfriend of Samantha Matero and current love interest of Lina Coleman."

"Do you mean that Lina and Samantha are rivals on *and* off the running field?" Nancy said, surprised.

"Big time!" Paul said.

George leaned forward, resting her elbows on her knees. "But I don't get it," she said. "What's this got to do with Samantha's extracurricular activities and Coach Abrams?"

"According to the grapevine, Coach thought Samantha was spending too much time with Matthew and not enough in training. She was late for practices, sometimes just didn't show. She and Matt were really a hot item at the beginning of the year," he explained. "Samantha thought she could coast along on her natural talent. Coach Abrams thought differently—team spirit, discipline, and all that. He put her on probation. When he called a practice, he expected everyone to be there, including his star runner." Paul looked from Nancy to George. "So what's your big interest in all this?"

Nancy quickly covered for herself and George. "We tried out for cross-country this afternoon and were wondering about track safety. We'd heard something about accidents, and then Lina told us that Samantha was faking her injury."

A frown briefly crossed Paul's face and then quickly disappeared behind a charming grin. "Oh, I don't think Samantha would do that," he said, standing up. He touched Nancy's shoulder lightly. "I've got to go. I'll see you tomorrow. Four o'clock?"

"Perfect," Nancy replied.

She watched as he jogged off toward the parking lot, and turned back to find George staring at her.

"What?" Nancy asked.

"You're pulling a Bess on me," George said with a grin.

Nancy blushed. "Not quite," she retorted.

Bess Marvin, George's cousin and Nancy's other best friend, was famous for falling in and out of love without warning. She often helped Nancy with her cases, but right now she was away for two weeks, visiting family.

"I wasn't sure it was smart to let Bess go off to romantic Niagara Falls, even to stay with relatives," George grumbled. She looked up and smiled. "And now I have to worry about you."

Nancy laughed and flipped her hair over her shoulder. "You've got to admit, he's cute."

"He is that," George said as they walked back into the building. "What now?"

"Now we go and find Samantha. She's the only one with the answers. I hope she's still here. The gym and the weight room are open till six."

A moment later George stuck her head in the weight room and looked around. "She's not there," she reported. "The place is deserted, except for Miss Raccoon Eyes."

Nancy grinned at the apt description of Lina. "Let's try the locker room," she suggested.

They found Samantha there, gathering her things to leave.

"Good workout?" George asked her.

"*No* workout," Samantha replied angrily. "I left the weight room the minute Lina Coleman showed up. I've been sitting in here waiting for her to go, but it's obvious she's going to stay until they lock the room. She's taking her time because she knows I'm waiting."

"Sam," Nancy said. "Sit down for a minute. There's some stuff we have to clear up before I can do anything to help you."

Samantha rested her book bag on the bench, but she didn't sit down. "What stuff?" she asked, leaning on her crutches and looking at the floor.

"Well, I wish you had told me that Coach Abrams had put you on probation," Nancy said. "And about Matthew."

"Matthew is my business!" Samantha snapped. "Who have you been talking to? Lina? I suppose she told you that I'm faking my injury, too. She spread *that* lie all over school. Well, I'm not! You can ask anybody else on the team if you really want to know. But it's not any of your business, anyway. You're supposed to be investigating the athletic department, not me!" She snatched up her book bag and awkwardly pushed her way out of the locker room, almost colliding with Lina, who was coming in.

With a smirk on her face Lina stepped aside. "Okay to use the weights now, Matero," she called after her in a sarcastic voice. "I'm leaving."

But Samantha walked out of the locker room without looking back.

Lina shrugged and headed to the showers.

Nancy and George exchanged a look. There was definitely no love lost between Brookline's two top runners.

"Let's check the weight room," Nancy said as she heard the rush of water starting. "Maybe someone else is working out now. I'd like a second opinion about Samantha's injury."

"Sorry, nobody home," George said, leading the way into the empty room. She walked around inspecting the machines. "But they have pretty nice equipment. You want to check it out?"

"Might as well," Nancy said. "It doesn't look as though this investigation is going anywhere at the moment." She stopped at the bench press, straddled the bench, lay on her back, and reached overhead for the bar. "Spot for me, will you, George?"

"You bet."

As Nancy lifted the weights from the rack, she felt the bench shift under her with a creak. Was it her imagination, or did the setup seem not quite right? After a moment, though, she felt steadier, and eased the bar through a couple of presses, the heavy weights challenging her muscles.

"That's enough for now," she said to George after five repetitions. She set the weights carefully back on the rack and said, "Thanks."

"Any time," George replied, turning to look at a row machine.

Suddenly there was the grinding squeal of metal on metal. George whirled around and Nancy screamed—as the bench collapsed and the weights went down with a sickening thud.

Chapter Four

NANCY SAT on the floor, head in her hands, trying to catch her breath. Only her quick move to the side had saved her from certain injury.

White-faced, George squatted beside her. "Are you okay?" she asked in a trembling voice. "I'm sorry. I should have stayed with you."

Nancy shook her head. "No, it wasn't your fault. I told you I was through." She took a deep breath to calm herself and said, "I thought it felt unsteady. I should have checked it."

Running footsteps in the hall made Nancy look up. Sheila Keenan entered the room.

"I was in the gym and heard the scream. Are you all right?" the coach asked, rushing over to Nancy. "What happened?"

"I'm fine," Nancy said. With help from

George, she gingerly stood up and checked her arm, which was red and raw from where she had scraped it on the floor. "It startled me more than anything. The bench just gave out under me. Everything came down."

Sheila Keenan's eyebrows furrowed as she moved to check the equipment. "Metal stress," she murmured. "Nancy, would you like to go over to the emergency room and have a doctor check that arm?"

Nancy shook her head. "No, I'm really okay, thanks."

"Strange," the coach said, almost to herself. "I'll have all the equipment checked first thing tomorrow, before there's another accident. For now, I'm locking the room up." She hustled them out into the hall and said, "Good night, girls."

"She's right about its being strange," Nancy said as they watched Ms. Keenan go into her office. "But that was no accident."

George nodded. "I checked out that bench press, and there was no metal stress. The nuts looked as if they'd been deliberately loosened from the bolts!"

The girls gathered their things from the empty locker room and walked out to the parking lot.

"Two questions," George said. "Who? And why?" She shifted her backpack to one side. "Lina, to cause injury to Samantha . . . ?"

"Or—and I hate to even think this," Nancy

said as she unlocked the passenger door. "Was it Samantha, trying to injure Lina? Samantha said she was in the weight room and left when Lina came in. She could have been waiting around to see what would happen."

"That would be a horrible thing to do," George said, snapping the seat belt in place.

"Yeah," Nancy agreed as she pulled out into traffic. "The interesting thing is that they both have the same motives. A cross-country scholarship—and Matthew Lee."

"Suppose it wasn't either Samantha or Lina?" George countered. "Keenan looked at that bench and didn't seem at all surprised. Surely she could see that it had been tampered with."

Nancy nodded. "Yes, but she didn't want to call it to our attention. Maybe she was afraid she'd be accused of negligence—like Coach Abrams. Maybe it wasn't intended for anyone in particular. It could have been done to put another black mark on the athletic department. Although I can't think of a reason."

"To make sure the team's disqualified by the district?" George offered.

"Maybe." Nancy veered into the right lane and turned the corner. "Let's see if there are any runners at Java Village," she said. "I still want to talk to someone who was on the track the day Samantha hurt her ankle."

The coffeehouse, just a couple of blocks from the school, was clearly a favorite hangout of students. The upbeat sounds of Workhorse, a local rock group, filled the room as they entered. A girl waved at them from a table in the rear.

"She's in my English class. Her name's Katy Marks," Nancy explained to George as they made their way back.

Other students at the table crowded their chairs together to make room for Nancy and George.

"How did your tryouts go?" Katy asked.

"Keenan's posting the roster tomorrow afternoon," Nancy said. "We've got our fingers crossed."

"You'll make it," Katy said. "It'll be great to have you both on the team." She grinned at George. "I'm looking forward to taking you on."

"It's a deal," George replied, giving her a high five.

Amy Swan and another girl at the table, Deirdre McCall, both on the cross-country team, began to discuss the athletic department's problems. "Only the brave try out for cross-country!" Dierdre said with a laugh.

"The team's had its problems with accidents, I hear," Nancy said.

"We've lost a few runners along the way," Amy volunteered. "Torn ligaments, shin splints, sprains, that kind of stuff. Let's face it. If you're going to go out for cross-country, you've got to be tough. And you have to really want to run. The dropouts didn't want it badly enough."

"Somebody told me this morning that Samantha was faking her injury," Nancy said.

Amy rolled her eyes and took a deep breath. "I hate to stick up for Matero after all the trouble she's caused the athletic department, but I was right behind her when she went down, and her ankle really was torn up."

Deirdre and the girl sitting next to her nodded in agreement. "Nobody's happy about the way her dad went after Coach Abrams, but she's not faking her injury," Deirdre said. "There was a hole in the track, but it wasn't Abrams's fault."

"I heard that Abrams was too tough on his runners," George said.

"He was strict," Amy agreed. "But he got results. And he was fair."

One thing seemed very clear to Nancy as she listened. Daniel Abrams, despite his reputation as a tough coach, was well liked and respected by the students.

"What do you think, Matt?" asked Katy, turning to catch the arm of a dark-haired, solemn-faced student walking past the table. She gestured toward Nancy and George. "Matthew Lee . . . Nancy Drew and George Fayne."

Matthew nodded at Nancy and George and turned back to Katy. "What do I think about what, Katy?" he asked.

"We're talking about Abrams. Where would you rank him as a coach, on a scale of one to ten?" Katy asked. "Matt plays basketball," she explained to Nancy and George. "Abrams was the assistant basketball coach as well as track coach."

"As a coach, the man's an eleven," Matthew said without hesitation. "He's wasted teaching freshman English. It's totally bogus." The bitterness in his voice was obvious.

Matthew turned away, and Nancy watched him weave through the crowded coffee shop to the front entrance.

"He's really a nice guy," Amy said, almost apologetically.

"Nice guy, short fuse," Deirdre added.

"True," Amy said. "He's famous for his explosions. What I can't figure out is what he sees in Lina."

"That's easy. It's get-even time," Deirdre said. "Samantha broke up with him, so he dates her rival to get back at her. Plus, now he's ticked off because of what the Materos did to Abrams. What better way to hurt Sam than to make her jealous?"

Nancy and George stayed another ten minutes and then made their way out to the car.

"So that blows one theory," George said as they drove into the outskirts of River Heights. "Amy convinced me that Samantha's injury is real."

"Me, too," Nancy added, braking for a red light. "And Deirdre verified what she said."

"I guess it makes sense that Matthew would

date Lina to get even with Samantha. Especially if he's got the temper they say he has," George said.

Nancy nodded. "And if he's that much of a hothead, he might be getting even in other ways, too."

"Like phone calls, and threatening notes," George said. "And the weight-room tampering."

Nancy sighed. "Yeah," she said. "We sure don't have a shortage of motives in this case." A moment later she pulled up in front of George's house. "See you in the morning," she said.

"Right," George replied. "There's a downside to being back in school. Homework."

Nancy grimaced as she drove off, thinking about some studying she had ahead of her, too. But even more important, she had to figure out how to approach Samantha in the morning. Without her cooperation, they'd never solve the case—a case that was getting more dangerous by the day. Following the weight-room scare, Nancy was convinced that someone was deliberately creating the danger at Brookline High.

The next morning Samantha was waiting in the hall at Nancy's locker when George and Nancy arrived.

"Think we're in for more fireworks?" George asked quietly as they approached her.

Nancy didn't know what to expect.

"Look," Samantha said awkwardly, before

they even greeted her. "I'm sorry about losing my temper last night. You were right. I should have told you that Abrams put me on probation. My dad doesn't even know about it, and I wanted to keep it from him." Samantha put a hand to her cheek and said, "I feel terrible that Abrams got pulled from the athletic department. I swear, that's not what I expected to happen."

Nancy started to reply, but Samantha went on, clearly upset. "And my breakup with Matt, and then his dating Lina . . . My whole life has been upside down. But I'm not making up my injury! And something *is* wrong in the athletic program here."

The shrill warning bell interrupted her, and Nancy reached over and touched her arm. "I know you're not lying about your injury," she assured her. "And I agree that something is wrong at Brookline. Meet us for lunch. We'll talk more."

At lunchtime the girls took their yogurt out under a shade tree near the track, distancing themselves from the other students.

"So what happened between you and Matthew?" Nancy asked, stretching out on the grass. "We heard you were the one who broke it off."

"That's right," Samantha whispered. "After Coach Abrams put me on probation, I just said that we should cool it for a while. But Matt didn't know I was on probation. I wanted to tell him the whole story, but he didn't give me a chance." Her voice cracked. "He just stormed off. He avoided me at school, and when I phoned his house to try to explain, he hung up on me. A week later he started dating Lina."

"Do you and Matt ever talk to each other now?" George asked.

"No!" Samantha said. "I avoid all of them—Lina, Matt, and Abrams."

"I still haven't met Abrams," Nancy said, half to herself. "I'm curious about him." She turned her attention back to Samantha. "Look, let's shift gears," she said. "Going back to yesterday afternoon, you said you went into the weight room and then left when Lina arrived. Right?"

Samantha nodded.

"Did you notice what equipment she was working on?"

"She was on the leg curl machine when I left."

"Not the bench press?"

"No, she concentrates on her legs, mostly. One of the guys may have been on the bench press. There were a half dozen in there before Lina came."

"Who?" Nancy asked.

Samantha frowned as she tried to remember. "Robby Kendrick, Paul Johnson, Sam Cohen, Matt . . . I really don't remember. I just tried to ignore them. They're all really mad at me."

"Speaking of Paul Johnson," said George, turning to Nancy. "I notice that you're wearing a new top today. For your big date?"

Nancy blushed and looked down at her print leggings and blue velour top.

"Do you know Paul?" Samantha asked.

"I met him yesterday," Nancy explained. "In the parking lot. Before I'd been here even five minutes! And I have a date with him this afternoon."

"That's Paul." Samantha laughed. "He doesn't let any grass grow under his feet when there's a pretty girl around."

"He seems older than most of the kids here," George said. "At least, that's the impression I got."

"He is," Samantha said. "He bummed around Europe most of last year and came back to school to make up two subjects that he needs to get into Beaverton. Paul's a little flaky but totally fun. Not to mention wicked cute!"

Nancy grinned. "I noticed," she said.

George whistled through her teeth. "He wants to go to Beaverton?" she said. "That takes brains. And money."

"You're right," Samantha agreed. "It's pretty pricey and a definite challenge academically. Even a high SAT score doesn't guarantee you'll get in. They do a whole series of independent preadmit tests. The first one comes up this

Saturday. If Paul doesn't pass it, he won't even get to take the second one."

"Ugh," George said. "One exam is bad enough. Why would anyone want to take more?"

"Well," Samantha said, "Beaverton is his uncle's alma mater. Paul told me there was a condition on his inheritance. He'll lose a block of stock if he's not admitted."

"Nothing like a little motivation." George laughed as she stood up. "Should we head back? You know I'd hate to miss physics."

The afternoon passed slowly for Nancy. She saw Paul from a distance between classes, and he held up four fingers to remind her when their date was, then disappeared into the lab. She smiled and nodded, aware that her pulse was beating more rapidly than usual and her cheeks were flushed with color. Calm down, Drew, she told herself. You're on a case here, not a date! But she couldn't help looking forward to coffee that afternoon.

When the last class ended, Nancy and Samantha met in the hall and walked toward their lockers. George was already flinging stuff into hers, and when she saw them coming, she gave Nancy a victory salute. "The cross-country list is up in the gym!" she yelled. "You made it!"

"All right!" Samantha cheered, beaming at Nancy. "That's great. Congratulations." But her smile quickly turned into a somber expression. She nudged Nancy with her elbow. "That's him," she whispered. "Coach Abrams. You were curious."

A stocky man with closely cropped dark hair and the rigid posture of a military officer stood at the far end of the bank of lockers. He stared at them for a moment before striding off in the opposite direction.

"He'll never get a job on the Welcome Wagon," George said.

Samantha smiled at George's attempt at humor. "He's still furious with me and my dad. I wish things hadn't . . ." She looked away and shrugged, then said, "Oh, well. Can't change what's already happened."

Samantha moved toward her locker and reached for the combination lock. "That's weird," she muttered. The lock was hanging loosely from the hasp, and the door was slightly ajar.

Samantha opened her locker—and gasped. Nancy quickly moved to her side.

The locker had been trashed. Books were torn, and notebook pages balled up and scattered. A white sheet of paper was wedged into the vents at the top of the metal door.

Samantha reached up and pulled the paper out. Her face drained of color, and with a trembling hand she passed the note to Nancy. The words were crudely printed in the familiar heavy black felt pen that Nancy remembered from the last note Samantha had received. The message was framed within a poorly drawn picture of a movie theater marquee:

COMING SOON!
YOUR NEXT ACCIDENT!!

Chapter Five

TEARS WELLED UP in Samantha's eyes and spilled down her cheeks. The hall was filling with students eager to leave at the end of the day. Several at nearby lockers cast curious glances in Samantha's direction when they realized she was crying, but before any questions could be asked, George had slammed the locker door shut and replaced the padlock. Nancy quickly put a comforting arm around Samantha's shoulder, and they led her down the hall and into the back of the now deserted cafeteria.

"I am so sick of this mess," Samantha sobbed. "I don't know why he's doing this to me."

"Who?" Nancy asked gently. "Mr. Abrams?" The image of the ex-coach by the lockers and his hasty retreat flashed through her mind.

Samantha looked startled, then shook her head. "No, not Abrams. Matt!"

"Matt?" Nancy asked, glancing at the crudely scratched note. "Do you recognize his writing?"

"No," Samantha replied. She blew her nose and took a deep breath. "It doesn't look like his writing, but he has to be behind it. He was really mad at me for breaking up with him. And then he got even madder when Coach Abrams was replaced."

Nancy raised a quizzical eyebrow. "Are those strong enough motives to threaten you?" she asked.

"I don't know," Samantha replied. "Nothing makes sense anymore." She blew her nose again. "And he's probably thinking about Lina. Now that the team may not be able to compete, she won't have a chance at a scholarship, either."

"Don't worry, Sam. You're in good hands," Nancy said. "George and I will get to the bottom of this." She glanced at her watch. "Right now I have a date at Java Village . . . and you have a date with your doctor. Good luck!"

"I'm going into River Heights, George," Samantha said. "Can I give you a lift?"

George took Samantha up on her offer, and the three of them walked in silence to the parking lot, each absorbed in her own thoughts.

Nancy pulled into a parking space at Java Village and spotted Paul's shiny Jeep Cherokee right away. It was almost as flamboyant as its owner, she thought as she glanced into her visor mirror to check her hair and makeup.

Nancy entered the restaurant and stood for a moment inside the door, searching for Paul. He was seated alone in a booth off to the side, and he stood up as she approached. His warm greeting made her feel a little giddy, and she slid in on the bench as he sat down opposite.

"I've been looking forward to this all day," Paul said. He beckoned to a waiter and quickly ordered for them. "And I understand that you had a nice surprise today."

Nancy, her mind still reeling with thoughts of the note in Samantha's locker, gave him a puzzled look.

"The list is up in the gym," Paul continued, "and you and George both made the team. Maybe we can do some training together."

"Oh, right," Nancy replied. "Thanks. I didn't know you were a runner, Paul."

Paul's eyes crinkled at the corners as he smiled across the table at her. "I'm not one of the superstars, but I'm on the team. I do just enough to keep me in shape. Besides running, I do weights almost every day."

"So were you in the weight room yesterday?" Nancy asked.

"Briefly," Paul replied. "I spotted for Matt Lee for a while, then got out of there. Lucky thing, too. As I was leaving, I saw Lina heading in, and I try never to get caught in the crossfire between her and Samantha." Paul drummed his fingers on the tabletop in time to the music blaring from the loudspeaker. "Why? Did you go in after I left?"

Nancy nodded. "I just missed a total disaster in there," she said. "The nuts had been loosened from the bolts on the bench press. The whole thing hit the floor. I was lucky to get out of the way in time."

Paul instantly reached across the table and took her hand. Nancy felt a tingle as his strong fingers curled around hers. "Nancy, that's terrible," he said, the concern in his voice matching the worried look on his face. "I wish all these accidents would stop. It's like the whole athletic department is jinxed."

"Well, it wasn't an accident," Nancy said. "It was deliberate."

Paul leaned forward. "I hope you reported it."

"I didn't have to. Sheila Keenan came running in when she heard me scream. She was planning to have all the equipment checked today."

"Smart move," Paul said, giving her hand another squeeze.

Nancy leaned back in the booth and tilted her head as she looked at Paul. "So," she said, "tell me about Paul Johnson. Samantha says you're headed for Beaverton next fall, and that you spent last year in Europe."

Paul stretched his long legs out on the seat and

settled his back up against the wall. "You're quite a little sleuth, aren't you?" he said, grinning as he studied her.

Nancy's easy smile hid the red flag that went up in her mind at the word *sleuth*. She'd have to be careful not to give away her real reason for being at Brookline. If her identity became known—even to someone like Paul—she wouldn't be able to help Samantha.

"Just doing my homework," she replied.

"Commendable," Paul said, giving her a playful thumbs-up. "Let's start with Europe." He leaned his head back and closed his eyes, as if bringing back pleasant memories. "Europe was a blast. I bummed around from hostel to hostel, mostly in Spain and France. Met some terrific people and had some great adventures."

"Were you working or an exchange student or what?"

"I picked up odd jobs here and there—washing dishes, waiting on tables, that kind of stuff. I spent eleven months just traveling around. I'm lucky, though. I have a trust fund that gave me a cushion. Could have stayed there forever, but . . ."

"But?" Nancy prompted.

"But I had to come back and finish off two classes for my senior year, or I couldn't apply to Beaverton." Paul stroked his chin and looked off into space. "Beaverton," he murmured. "Beaverton College is a family tradition. My grandfather, my father, and my uncle are all Beaverton alumni. It's not my first choice in schools." His voice held a trace of bitterness.

"Then why go there?" Nancy asked.

"There's too much riding on it."

"I don't understand," she said, giving him a quizzical look.

"My late uncle put a condition in his will," Paul explained. "A large block of very valuable stock will go to me, on condition that I graduate from Beaverton. If I don't, the stock will go to the school endowment fund. So I have to jump through the hoops."

"Oh," Nancy murmured. She paused. "Maybe it's not worth it. . . ."

"Oh, it's worth it," Paul said. "Almost anything is worth a hundred thousand dollars."

Nancy's eyes widened. "A hundred thousand!"

Paul nodded and then grinned. He reached across the table to touch her hand again. "Can I order something else for you?" he asked.

Nancy glanced up at the clock over the coffee bar. "No, thanks. I've got to get going. Lots of homework tonight."

"I'll walk you to your car," Paul said, taking her arm.

When they reached the Mustang, he took the keys from her hand and, after unlocking the door, turned to encircle her in his arms. He gazed into Nancy's eyes for a moment, then slowly lowered his head and planted a kiss firmly on her lips.

A delicious warm feeling coursed through Nancy's body as she returned the kiss and then leaned back to look at him.

Paul's dark eyes were dancing, and he chuckled, a low sound from deep in his throat. "I'll see you tomorrow, Nancy Drew," he said, opening the door for her. "Maybe at lunch. And save me Friday night!" he added. "Party time!"

"Sounds great," Nancy said, getting into the car. "See you tomorrow."

She hummed along with the stereo as she pulled out into traffic. Lunch tomorrow. Party on Friday. She definitely had a good week ahead!

The next day George and Nancy stood in line together in the crowded school cafeteria, quietly comparing thoughts about the trashing of Samantha's locker.

"Paul told me that Matt was one of the guys in the weight room on Monday," Nancy said, looking across the room at Matt. He was sitting alone at a corner table, reading a book.

"That puts him in line as a possible suspect," George said, following Nancy's gaze. "Along with Lina, and maybe Abrams."

"Speaking of Lina," Nancy said. The girls watched as Lina approached Matthew from behind and coyly covered his eyes with her hands. Matthew's reaction was immediate. He jerked his head free and looked over his shoulder to see who was behind him. With an angry glare he spoke briefly and then turned away. Clearly annoyed, Lina swung around and marched to a table where some of her friends were seated.

"What do you make of that?" George asked. "Lovers' quarrel?"

Nancy's forehead wrinkled in a frown. "I don't know. Maybe it's just Matt's short fuse again. Samantha thinks he's really serious about Lina, but seeing that incident makes me wonder." She and George paid the cashier and surveyed the room for an empty table. "Let's get that table beside Lina. Maybe we'll hear something," Nancy suggested.

Five minutes later a smiling Samantha—without crutches—came through the line and, with one quick glare at Lina's back, joined them.

"Good news!" she said. "The doctor says I can go back into modified training, and if the ankle holds, I'll be able to run in the race next week. Not that I expect even to place, but I need to get started again."

"That's great," George said. "There's practice this afternoon. We'll see you on the course."

Nancy, with her attention on Matthew, only half heard the conversation. Matthew was walking toward them, unsmiling, staring at Samantha.

Samantha followed Nancy's gaze, and a look of panic crossed her face. She lowered her eyes to the salad in front of her. But Matthew wasn't coming to their table. Walking past them, he stopped at Lina's side and squatted near her chair. Then he put his arm around her waist possessively. A quiet exchange of words followed before a smiling Matt left the cafeteria, with Lina gazing lovingly after him.

"I hate them both," Samantha said, crumpling a napkin in her fist.

George's eyes were wide with disbelief at the scene. "If it's any consolation," she said, "he gave her the royal brush-off just ten minutes ago."

"I'm getting out of here," Samantha announced shakily as she stood up.

"Good idea," Nancy said. "I'd go with you, but Paul said he might show up."

"I'll take a walk with you, Sam," George offered. "See you later, Nancy."

Nancy nodded, glad that George had recognized the quiver in Samantha's voice as a prelude to an emotional scene. "Right. I'll hang out in case Paul comes. He wasn't in history this morning."

Nancy watched as Lina's group broke up and pondered the sudden change in Matthew's attitude. Had the tender gestures and conversation with Lina been real? Was he trying to make up for giving Lina the brush-off earlier? Or was he only trying to make Samantha jealous?

Just as Nancy gave up on waiting for Paul, he

entered the cafeteria. Smiling at her from the doorway, he hurried to her table and straddled a chair. "Sorry I'm late," he said. "I had an errand to run and it took longer than I thought."

"No problem," Nancy said, returning his smile. "Aren't you going to eat?"

"No time before class," he replied, looking at his watch. "I'll get something later."

The cafeteria was clearing out as the students headed to their classrooms. Nancy glanced up in response to a greeting from Amy Swan, who was leaving, and noticed Sheila Keenan striding quickly toward their table. Nan could tell by the way she moved that she was angry.

The moment she reached them, Ms. Keenan launched into a tirade. Eyes flashing, hands on her hips, she faced Paul.

"I've had it, Mr. Johnson!" she announced. "No more! One more thing and that's it! And I expect you to show up for *every* class. Understand?"

With that, the coach turned and marched out of the cafeteria, without giving Paul a chance to reply.

Chapter Six

"WHOA," NANCY SAID, looking at Paul with surprise.

He waved his hand in a dismissive gesture and stood up. "Cheerful mood she's in today," he said sarcastically. "Ready?" He picked up Nancy's books and moved her chair back as she stood up. "Remind me not to cut history again," he added lightly.

"You'd better not," Nancy warned him as the bell rang. "See you later, Paul." With a brief wave, Nancy hurried into her next classroom.

Nancy figured it must be hard for Paul—someone who'd already had a year of independence in Europe—to have to come back to a small-town high school and toe the line. And yet that was the choice he'd made. Nobody had forced him to do it. If he wanted his full inheritance, graduation was one of the steps to getting it.

Nancy's thoughts were interrupted as the class began. With a sigh she turned her attention to schoolwork.

The cross-country practice at the end of the day was arduous, with Coach Keenan directing the team to run sprints up and down Mount Fuji, followed by a six-mile jog. Samantha's workout was restricted to less than half that of the regular runners.

Paul had already completed the run and was stretching out with George near the bleachers when Nancy came in off the course.

"Come take a walk with me," he suggested, draping an arm over her shoulders.

Nancy grinned up at him and blew the hair out of her eyes. "Just what I need," she panted. "A little exercise."

"Ah, come on," he coaxed. "Just a short walk out to the pond. I want to ask you properly for a date."

Nancy looked over at George.

"I've got studying to do," George said, making a face. "Physics again. And I told Samantha I'd meet her. We'll be in the library."

Paul took Nancy's hand. Swinging their arms, the two of them walked from the playing field into the woods, heading for Pitfall Pond. The beautiful afternoon had a warm, lazy feel that was almost like summer, except for the colorful splash of autumn leaves.

"Gorgeous day!" Nancy said, flopping down on the gentle grassy slope that bordered the water. The fading light of the late afternoon sun was creating golden streaks on the still surface of the pond.

"Gorgeous girl," Paul said softly, propping himself up on an elbow beside her. He put an arm gently on her shoulders and lifted her long hair aside, trailing his fingers lightly on the nape of her neck.

Nancy's breath caught in her throat. She raised her eyes to Paul's as he drew her close and kissed her . . . a warm kiss that made her heart beat like a tom-tom.

Nancy sat up and tried to shake off the spinning sensation in her head. "I thought we were going to talk," she teased.

"Oh, we are," Paul said, with a grin. "We're going to talk about you coming to a party that I'm giving on Friday night."

"What's the occasion?" Nancy asked.

"Nothing special. We could call it a prerace party, since the big meet for the women's team is coming up next week. My folks are in Mexico this month, and our big house gets plenty quiet. I thought we could liven it up a little. It'll be mostly runners. George and Samantha are invited, too."

"Speaking of George and Samantha, I'd better

get back." Nancy jumped up and offered Paul her hand, but instead of getting up, he pulled her back down and planted another kiss on her lips.

"There's one for the road," he said, laughing.

On the way back Nancy stopped and pointed out the place where Samantha had taken her fall. "She thinks someone deliberately dug the hole."

"Why would anyone do that?" Paul asked, dismissing the idea. "You're beginning to sound like her bodyguard." He stooped to retie one of his shoelaces. "How do you like Coach Keenan?"

Nancy shrugged. "I haven't been here long enough to make a judgment—except for her performance in the cafeteria today."

Paul brushed aside the comment. "I meant her coaching style, not her manners. She's a lot different from Abrams," Paul said. "I don't think she's as good."

"That may be a gender thing," Nancy said as they entered the school. "A lot of guys aren't comfortable with women coaches."

"You may be right," Paul said. "Well, I'm off to the showers. See you tomorrow. And don't forget about Friday night, eight-ish."

"I won't," Nancy said, before heading toward the library.

Samantha and George gathered up their papers as Nancy approached, and together they walked back to the locker room. It was empty when they got there.

"You didn't have to leave right away," Nancy

said. "I just wanted to let you know I was back. I still have to take a shower."

"I've had enough headwork for one day," Samantha said. "I'll do something simple in the weight room until you're ready. Get some endorphins going."

Nancy looked quickly at George. Samantha had not been told about the accident with the bench.

"I'll go with you," George said. "When Nan is ready, we can go and get something to eat."

"Food sounds fantastic," Nancy said as she tugged on the door to her gym locker. "Whoa, maybe I should do some weight training, too," she said. "I can't get this door open. My towel is in here, but I don't seem to have enough strength to get this door unstuck."

Gritting her teeth and putting both hands on the handle, Nancy gave a final, forceful yank.

"Look out!" George yelled.

Nancy looked up and gasped. The entire bank of lockers was falling toward her!

Chapter Seven

NANCY DIVED to the right, narrowly escaping the lockers as they fell. The room reverberated with a shattering crash as the lockers hit the floor. It had all happened so fast that Nancy sat for a moment, stunned, on the floor where she'd landed. Many hands helped her to her feet; on one side, she was flanked by a shaken Samantha and George, on the other by Sheila Keenan.

"Man coming in!"

Everyone turned to see a school custodian burst through the double doors, closely followed by Paul. "Sounded like a plane came through the roof," the custodian said, looking with dismay at the fallen lockers. "Glad you weren't hurt, miss."

"Are you okay?" Paul asked Nancy, his face a somber mask of concern. He put his arm around her waist and led her over to a bench.

"This is no coincidence," Nancy said grimly.

Sheila Keenan, her face drained of color, stared at Nancy. "It was negligence," she said quickly. "Maintenance repainted the floor in here. Obviously, the lockers were not securely refastened when they were put back."

"But they were," the custodian retorted. "Mr. Abrams can vouch for that. He came in the night I was doing it and helped me brace them up against the wall." The custodian crawled around behind the lockers to check the braces. "Looks to me as if someone cut these bolts."

Sheila Keenan grew even paler but did not respond. "Okay," she said finally. "Everybody out. There's nothing we can do here. Paul, you help Mr. Carruthers prop these back up."

"Sure. Be glad to," Paul said.

Nancy gathered her things and said goodbye to Paul. Then she, George, and Samantha followed Sheila Keenan out of the locker room.

The coach looked quizzically at Nancy as they walked down the hall. Outside her office, she stopped and said, "Strange how you transfer students always seem to be right in the thick of the action here at Brookline," she said. She entered the room and closed the door before Nancy could reply.

"What was that all about?" Samantha asked. "She sounded very suspicious. Does she know that you're investigating?"

Nancy took a deep breath. "I don't think so. Let's go and get a pizza and I'll explain."

"I'll take my own car and meet you there," Samantha replied.

The pizza parlor was just a mile from the school and surprisingly quiet for that time of day. The girls found a booth in the back, and Samantha slipped into the seat facing Nancy and George.

"Before we get into the heavy stuff," Nancy said, "how would you like some good news?"

"Let's hear it," George said. "I'm ready!"

"Paul is having a party on Friday night," Nancy went on. "And you're both invited."

"Does he have any collapsing walls at his place?" George joked. "If so, I'll pass."

Nancy smiled. "No, I don't think so. You'll be safe."

"Friday night?" Samantha repeated. "He's nuts. That's the night before the Beaverton College test. I can't believe he's throwing a party."

Nancy shrugged. "Maybe the test was rescheduled. I know he said Friday."

They placed their order, and when the waiter left the table, Samantha turned to Nancy. "Okay," she said. "Now the heavy stuff. Tell me why Coach Keenan said what she did about you."

Nancy sighed. "Sam, there was another accident earlier this week." She explained what had happened in the weight room. "We decided it was best not to tell you."

"Not tell me!" Samantha exclaimed. "Nancy, you could have been badly hurt. What day was it?"

"Monday. The day you were waiting for Lina to leave."

When Nancy finished explaining, Samantha leaned back and took a deep breath. "So Lina had plenty of time alone in there to set it up. And then she had the nerve to come and tell me she was leaving and that I could go in."

"We don't know that it was Lina who loosened the bench nuts," Nancy said. "All we know is that Keenan claimed it was metal stress, which it wasn't. It was definitely deliberate. Do you have any idea why Keenan would want to mislead us?"

"Covering up for the department, I guess. She doesn't want Brookline athletics to get another black mark. And she may be covering for Lina, too. She's the team's best runner now." Samantha's voice was bitter.

"It seemed like more than that," Nancy said. "What else do you know about Keenan?"

Samantha looked puzzled. "Well, she's been after me to get my dad to talk to his friends on the board again."

"To have the board convince the district to let the Brookline team compete?" George asked.

Samantha nodded.

"Did you talk to your dad?" Nancy asked.

"I tried. I talked to him about it last night."

"And?" Nancy said as the pizza arrived.

Samantha made a face. "You saw how my father acted in Mr. Drew's office. His whole life revolves around me. And he's afraid I'll get hurt again. I tried to convince him that it would be good for me to participate, and that I wouldn't push myself too hard, but he's stubborn. He wants me to compete, but not until he's *sure* it's safe." She paused. "Do *you* think the team should compete on Tuesday?"

"I don't know," Nancy answered. "It might put you at more risk. But on the other hand, it might give us the break in the case that we need. And since George and I are both on the team, we can keep an eye on you."

Samantha nibbled at the crust of her pizza. She hesitated, then said, "I'm beginning to wonder if having you two around puts me in more danger than before." She slid across the bench and stood up. "I've got to go. I'll see you tomorrow."

"I can't blame Samantha for being worried," Nancy said to George once Samantha had gone. "I just wish I could have been more reassuring."

"There's no good way to tell somebody that they're being targeted, Nan," George said. "If Samantha is the target." Suddenly she sat up straight. "Nan, what if *you're* the target? What if somebody has figured out who you are and why you're here? Keenan sounded as if she suspected something."

"Yes," Nancy agreed, "but she wouldn't be setting up accidents that would make her look bad. She just got the head coaching job when Abrams was suspended. She doesn't want to lose what could become a permanent position."

George slumped in her seat. "You're right," she said. "Okay, try this idea. What if Abrams cut the bolts? He knew how the lockers were secured because he helped the custodian put them back up. He also had motive. He must feel a lot of resentment toward Keenan. The so-called accident would reflect badly on her."

"True," Nancy said. "And in that case the accident wouldn't have been specifically intended for Samantha or me, but just anybody."

"Same with the bench in the weight room," George said, taking a sip of her soda. "But there's someone else we're not considering," she continued, arching an eyebrow. "Guess who."

Nancy sighed. "You mean Paul. He was in the weight room the day the bench collapsed. And today he showed up right after the lockers fell. But what's his motive?" She looked down at the table and bit her lip. "And maybe he did have an opportunity in the weight room. But, George, he was with me today, out at the pond right before the lockers fell. And when we came back, he went to take a shower. He's got a perfect alibi."

"Not a perfect alibi," George said slowly.

"Kind of hard to take a shower and keep your hair dry. Unless you put a bucket over your head."

Despite George's attempt at humor, Nancy's expression grew serious as the implication of the words sank in. "I didn't notice his hair," she said.

"You were too busy dodging falling lockers," George said. "But his hair was dry, bone dry."

There was a silence as the two friends sat contemplating. Finally, Nancy spoke. "Something else," she said. "After you and Sam left the cafeteria today, Keenan charged in and chewed out Paul about missing class this morning. It might be my imagination, but she was really angry—too angry about something as minor as a skipped class. I had the feeling she wanted to say more, but she didn't because I was there."

George rested her chin in her hands and looked thoughtful. "Nan, you know, I could be entirely wrong about Paul. I hope I am. I know you like him, and I may be way off base, but he *was* at the scene of two very suspicious incidents."

Nancy waved aside her explanation. "It's okay, George. You're right. I should know better than to ignore a possible suspect, just because I'm personally involved." She reached for her backpack on the bench beside her. "Maybe we'll hit on something Friday night at his party. As long as no one discovers our real reason for being at Brookline." She rose and slung her backpack over her shoulder. "Ready to go?"

The next day Nancy and Samantha met at their lockers and walked together to their first class.

"Anything new on the home front?" Nancy asked.

"No phone threats, if that's what you mean. And Dad said he'd think about talking to the school board again. I didn't tell him about the lockers falling on you."

"Smart move." Nancy grinned. "If you had, there's no way he'd consider asking the board to ease up." They reached Ms. Keenan's room and Nancy reached for the doorknob. "That's strange. The lights are on, but it's locked."

"You know, Dad mentioned something else last night," Samantha said, squinting through the door's narrow window. "He said that the two people who would benefit most if the team was allowed to compete would be Sheila Keenan and Lina Coleman. And look at this."

Inside the locked room the coach and Lina were engaged in what appeared to be a serious discussion. They were huddled in the corner, with their backs toward the door.

"Let's move down the hall," Samantha whispered. "I don't want to be the first one in there."

The bell rang. Nancy and Samantha held back, entering the room only with the last surge of students. Paul flashed his winning smile in Nancy's direction as he walked to his seat, and she responded once again to his charm, despite her conversation with George.

At the end of the period Sheila Keenan held up her hand in a brief signal for quiet. "Nancy Drew, please stay for a few minutes."

Surprised by the request, Nancy remained at her desk until the other students noisily filed out. When the last person left, Nancy walked to the front. Sheila Keenan closed the door and turned to Nancy, folding her arms in front of her.

"I've been told," she said, "that on Monday the district will rule on our team's admissibility to Tuesday's race. I think you realize that Brookline's athletic department is already under scrutiny, and I don't want to give the board or the district any more fuel for their fire." Her face set in hard lines, she looked directly at Nancy. "Which means that yesterday's incident in the locker room, and the earlier one in the weight room, must not be discussed with anyone. Is that understood?"

Nancy met the coach's gaze head on. "It's one thing to protect the department," she said boldly, "but not at the expense of student safety."

"Brookline students are quite safe," Ms. Keenan insisted. "You are mistaken if you think they're not. The things that occurred this week were *accidents*—the first resulting from misuse of equipment and the second from the maintenance department's negligence." Her eyes were cold as she stared at Nancy. "I expect you to tell your friend George not to talk about these incidents, too. There could be repercussions if either of you doesn't keep quiet. George is a talented runner. I doubt that you'd want to ruin her chance to compete. That's all, Nancy. You may leave."

Nancy bit her tongue as she headed for the door. She was turning the knob when the icy sound of Ms. Keenan's voice stopped her.

"Oh, and Nancy . . . should you break this trust, I will personally see to it that you are suspended from Brookline."

Chapter Eight

NANCY CLOSED THE DOOR behind her as she left Sheila Keenan's classroom, then stood in the hall for a moment to gather her thoughts. Coach Keenan's threat had taken her by surprise. Keenan had actually said she would suspend Nancy if she talked to anyone about the dangerous incidents that had happened during the past week.

That must mean only one thing, Nancy decided. Coach Keenan has something to hide. She doesn't want anyone to know what is going on in the athletic department.

Nancy began to make her way to the front steps, where she had planned to meet with George after class. Nancy found both George and Samantha waiting for her there and explained that she was late because she'd had words with Keenan.

"She's covering up something," Nancy said as they sat down on the steps. "I can understand why she wants the team to compete and why sabotage would throw a shadow on the department, but I don't think much of a coach who deliberately lies at the expense of her athletes. She *knows* they weren't accidents!"

"And she knows they could have harmed someone—seriously," George added. "You'd think she'd be more careful after what happened to Samantha. Keenan must really have something to hide, as you say, Nancy. Do you think it could have anything to do with that conversation she was having with Lina today in her classroom?"

"Possibly," Nancy said. "But I can't imagine what."

"I've got an idea," Samantha said. "My guess is that Keenan told Lina it could help the team if she were nice to me."

"I get it," George said. "Keenan thinks if your teammates are nice to you, you'll get your dad to talk to the board again. And then the board members would talk to the district and let us compete on Tuesday."

Samantha nodded. "Right. Lina just spoke to me in the hall in an unbelievably sweet tone of voice. She's so fake! I wanted to scream."

"I don't blame you," George said.

"At least Mr. Abrams treated all his runners alike," Samantha went on. "No favorites and no politics."

Nancy waited until a group of students passed by before speaking. "Sam, what are you going to do about Paul's party? He told me mostly runners would be there, and I have a hunch that both Lina and Matthew will be going."

Samantha leaned forward, resting her elbows on her knees. "I thought about that last night," she said, "and I decided that I had as much right to be there as anybody. I haven't done anything wrong. If my being there makes them uncomfortable . . . tough!"

George laughed. "Way to go, Sam!"

"I like your attitude," Nancy agreed, "but we also have to think about your safety. That party will be a gathering of your friends—and your enemies. The problem is that we don't know which is which. And since the district decision will be announced Monday, you may get the cold shoulder, or worse."

"I don't think Lina will pull anything," Samantha said. "She'll be on her best behavior until the Brookline team is cleared for competition. And she'll keep Matt in line for the same reason."

"What if Lina isn't the threat? Or Matthew?" Nancy said.

"Who else could it be?" Samantha asked. She

looked at her watch and stood up. "I've got a lab. See you at practice."

"Good question. Who else could it be?" George repeated, once Samantha had gone. "You can believe that I'll be sticking to Sam like glue tomorrow night." She grinned at Nancy. "I'm guessing that you'll be keeping a close eye on our host."

Nancy blushed. "True, but I'll try to make sure it's an unbiased eye. I'm not ruling out the fact that Paul's a possible suspect. Though I still can't imagine what his motive would be." She paused. "Do you have a class now?"

George nodded. "English. You?"

"Study period in the library," Nancy said as she poked around in her backpack. She pulled out the note that had been left in Samantha's locker. "Matthew Lee will be in there. I need to talk to him about this. I think he may know something."

"Good luck. See you at practice."

Nancy walked into the library and looked over the students in the study section. Matt was seated alone at a small table by the window.

"Is this seat taken?" she asked, approaching him. She motioned to the chair beside him.

"No," he replied, hastily removing his books from the chair.

"We met at Java Village earlier this week," Nancy reminded him as she sat down.

"I remember. You're Nancy Drew. I've seen you around school with Samantha Matero." Matthew's tone of voice was level, but his dark eyes were wary as he stared at Nancy, as if daring her to explain her friendship with Samantha.

Nancy met his gaze head on and decided to be blunt. "Samantha has received several threats since the team was told that it might be suspended."

"Her father's interference totally messed up the athletic department," Matthew said. "Daniel Abrams was the best coach that Brookline ever had, for cross country and men's basketball. Matero has wrecked more than one sports program in this school, and it's not right."

The librarian walked toward them, giving them a pointed glance, and Nancy opened a book and pretended to read until the woman had moved on. "That may be," she whispered. "But it's no excuse for someone to threaten Samantha." She took the note out of her pocket and slid it across the table toward Matthew. "Do you recognize this writing?"

Matthew's eyes flickered as he read the note, but at first he said nothing. A few seconds passed as he studied the piece of paper, his jaw clenched. Then he reached out and picked it up. "I'll take care of it," he said softly. Slipping the note inside one of his books, he abruptly stood up, grabbed his backpack, and strode away. He stopped long enough to be excused by the librarian in charge of study period, then disappeared into the hall.

Nancy leaned back in her chair, puzzled. The note had obviously disturbed Matthew. But was his reaction one of anger or guilt? Did he know who wrote the note, or had he written it himself? She stayed at the table, thinking, as the bell rang and the library cleared. Then she gathered her books and headed for the gym.

The light drizzle that started at lunchtime had turned into a steady rain by the time the runners gathered for practice in the gym.

"The track may be hazardous," Coach Keenan announced. "We'll stick to an inside workout today and hope that we'll get back on the course tomorrow." Nancy noticed that Coach Keenan pointedly avoided making eye contact with her or George as she spoke.

"I wonder where Paul is," Nancy said, looking over the group.

"Probably off planning his party," Samantha replied with a smile. "He's not really a serious runner, even though he's got a lot of talent."

Nancy peered through one of the gym's windows. Rain was sheeting from the sky, and here and there, shallow pools with green fringes of sodden grass had formed on the playing field.

Beyond the field, where the course entered into the woods, a raincoat-clad person strode determinedly through the rain and disappeared from view.

"Great day for a walk," George said, looking over Nancy's shoulder. "Who was it?"

"It looked like Coach Abrams," Nancy said. "I wonder where he's going."

"Drew! Fayne!" Sheila Keenan's voice was brittle as she came up behind them. "This is a workout, not a time to socialize. Ten extra gym laps at the end of the session."

Nancy and George fell into formation, running with the other team members to start the afternoon regime. Two hours later they'd finished their workout and taken showers.

"One thing you can say for penalty laps," George said as she combed her hair. "By the time you're done, the rush is over for the showers."

Nancy laughed as they left the locker room. "Big consolation." She stopped outside the closed door of Keenan's office, just off the gym, and waved at George to be quiet. "Paul's really pushing his luck with her," she whispered, looking through the door's narrow window. "He didn't show up for practice today." Inside the small room, Paul Johnson stood with his back turned toward the door as the coach yelled at him from across her desk.

"He looked like a drowned rat," George said as they moved down the hall. "I wonder why he was out in the rain."

"I don't know, but unfortunately, now it's our turn. I want to go out to the track and see if I can figure out what Abrams was doing. After that I'd like to take a look around Keenan's office. She should be leaving soon. Let's go to the car and get our rain gear."

"You're just full of terrific ideas," George grumbled good-naturedly as the steady downpour drummed against the roof.

The empty halls, usually filled with the chatter of students, were eerily silent as Nancy and George walked through the building. The sound of squealing tires halted them on the front steps, and a shiny black Jeep Cherokee came careening out of the parking lot.

"Paul," Nancy said, watching the car peel out to the street.

"He's either furious or in a heck of a hurry," George said.

Trying to avoid getting drenched, Nancy and George raced for the Mustang. Nancy unlocked the passenger side for George, who leaned across and unlocked the driver's side. Both girls collapsed in the front seat, glad to be in out of the rain.

"Doesn't a big, juicy hamburger with fries and a hot chocolate sound a lot better than a wet walk to Mount Fuji?" George teased.

Nancy laughed. "*After* the walk," she said, struggling into her raincoat. She reached for the door handle to climb out, but stopped suddenly. "Slouch down, George," she said. "Quickly."

Sheila Keenan appeared on the steps of the school, paused, and scurried for the teacher's parking area.

"Let's wait until she leaves," Nancy said.

"We're losing daylight," George pointed out. "If we're going to see anything on the track, we'll have to start soon."

"I know, but we haven't seen Keenan pull out. Let's wait."

"Maybe she drove out the other exit," George suggested.

Nancy looked at her watch and shook her head. "That gate is locked after five. George, look!" She straightened up and pointed toward the school. Sheila Keenan, now wearing a long raincoat, hat, and boots, climbed the steps and reentered the school.

"Well, look at that," George said. "She got raingear out of her car, just like us. Now where's she going?"

"Let's find out," Nancy replied. "My guess is that she's going to do the same thing we are. Come on."

The rain had slowly subsided to a drizzle, but gloomy clouds still hung overhead as they skirted the building and walked through the wet leaves and slippery grass toward the cross country course.

Suddenly Nancy grabbed George's arm and pointed across the playing field. They both watched Sheila Keenan's yellow raincoat disappear in the wooded area beyond the field.

"She must have gone in the front door and out the back," George whispered.

Cautiously they proceeded. Crouching close to the brush that lined the course, they rounded a curve. Ahead of them, the coach was on her hands and knees, methodically searching through a pile of wet leaves to the side of the course. Apparently satisfied that what she was looking for was not there, she moved to the other side of the path, probing at a bush.

What was she looking for? Nancy wondered. Was she also suspicious that someone might have booby-trapped the course? Keenan must have seen Abrams enter the woods earlier, when she and George saw him. Did she suspect the suspended coach of wrongdoing? Questions tumbled through her mind as the coach continued her search in the dim half-light of early evening.

Without warning the stillness was shattered by the raucous cawing of a crow, swooping into a huge oak tree.

Startled by the shrill noise, Keenan whirled around, instantly spotting Nancy and George, who had no time to hide.

The coach's face twisted with anger. "What are you doing here?" she demanded.

Chapter Nine

"SORRY WE STARTLED YOU," Nancy said to Coach Keenan. "When the rain eased up, we decided we'd walk the course one more time. . . ."

"To familiarize ourselves," George added.

"Can we help you look for something?" Nancy asked. "You seemed to be searching through the leaves."

Coach Keenan stared at them for a few seconds, her face frozen in an angry mask. She brushed some leaves from the front of her coat and then waved at the path just ahead. "I came out this morning before school started," she said, jamming her hands into her pockets, "to check the condition of the course. When I got to this point, I noticed that somehow I'd lost my ring."

She's lying, Nancy thought, watching closely as

the coach chose her words carefully. Keenan still had something to hide.

Ms. Keenan flashed an artificial smile. "The ring isn't valuable. It's silver and turquoise, something I got in New Mexico last summer. But it was a nice memento from my trip. It's like looking for a needle in a haystack."

"We'll help you look." George dropped to her knees and started on a pile of wet leaves.

"That's not necessary." Keenan's abrupt tone suggested she didn't want their help.

"No problem," Nancy said cheerfully as she, too, got to her knees.

The three of them worked their way down the course without talking, the two girls on one side and Coach Keenan on the other. A few minutes into the search there was a cry of triumph from the coach.

"I never thought I'd find it!" she gushed, holding up a handsome ring and then slipping it on her finger. "Thanks so much for helping me look, girls. I probably would have given up if you hadn't come along."

The charade was almost convincing, but Nancy knew better. However, she played along with Coach Keenan and said, "Glad to help. It would have been a shame to lose that nice ring."

"Nancy . . ." the coach said, and then paused. "I came down kind of hard on you this morning. I guess I'm just upset at all the things that have been happening. Anyhow, I'm sorry if I was too harsh. But I'd still appreciate it if both of you would not mention the accidents to anyone. I'll see you tomorrow." Without waiting for a reply, Coach Keenan turned and walked briskly back toward the school.

"Tricky the way she slipped her ring off and then miraculously found it under that bush," Nancy said when Keenan was out of earshot. "I wonder what she was *really* doing out here."

George shrugged. "I don't know. We're right back to where we started. That half-hearted apology to you was a surprise, too. What brought that on?"

"Coach Keenan knows we're friends of Samantha, and right now, Mr. Matero is the one person who can put the team back on the track—excuse the pun. So Keenan thinks she should get on our good side, because we have influence over Sam, and possibly her father."

The gray light of day was fading, and in wooded areas dark shadows fell across the path. George tripped over a tree root, and Nancy put out a hand to steady her.

"Thanks," George murmured.

They moved at a quick pace, eyes scanning the ground for any hazard on the course. Nancy kept her eyes trained on the left, and George took the right. Nothing appeared out of place until they reached Mount Fuji. They climbed the steep uphill side and started down the other, gaining speed on the descent.

"Hold it!" Nancy yelled. "Look over here." Nancy pointed to a two-foot-wide section of the slope covered with loose gravel. She bent down to inspect the area.

"This isn't rain washout," George said, brushing some gravel aside with her hand. "There's a mud-slick under this, and there's no loose gravel anywhere else on the course. I think it's been brought in."

"And any runner who was unlucky enough to hit that spot on the downhill run would take a nasty fall," Nancy added. "Which would probably happen tomorrow at practice."

"Let's go back," Nancy said after they had trampled the loose gravel into the mud until it was securely embedded. "I think we found what we were looking for."

"Now we just have to figure out *who* and *why,*" George added.

When they got back to the school, a funnel of light beamed through the window in Sheila Keenan's office door.

"Looks as if it's time to get those burgers," Nancy said quietly. "She's still here."

"Probably the only favor Coach Keenan will ever do for me," George said, dramatically clutching her stomach as they backed out of the building. "Saved me from sure starvation."

The restaurant was crowded and service was slow, but Nancy and George were in no hurry.

They wanted to give the coach plenty of time to leave the school. Almost an hour passed before the Mustang headed back into the Brookline High parking lot. The staff and faculty area was empty, except for the custodian's truck, and the student lot was deserted. Nancy pulled into a slot partially shadowed by the building and cut the motor.

"The front door will be locked," she said. "Let's see if we can get in through the back. Take the flashlight out of the glove compartment, will you?"

George grabbed the flashlight, and the two girls scurried to a side wall of the school, where they wouldn't be as visible.

"Piece of cake," George said as they rounded the corner of the building. The back door had been propped open to give the custodians easy access to the adjacent Dumpster.

Inside, minimal lights burned at the ends of the hallways, and the classrooms and offices were dark. A custodian's wheeled trash can was parked halfway down the corridor, and George and Nancy proceeded cautiously, not wanting to run into anyone who might pose questions. When they reached Sheila Keenan's office, Nancy tried the knob. Locked, as she had expected. She slipped a thin plastic card from her pocket and inserted it between the door frame and the lock, turning the knob as she gently applied pressure. The door opened quietly.

Once inside the small room George flicked on the flashlight and handed it to Nancy. "I'll watch the hall while you look around," she whispered, stationing herself to one side of the doorway, where she could look out the window in the door.

Quickly Nancy checked the papers neatly stacked on the desk. Sheila Keenan was orderly. Training manuals in one pile, academic papers in another. Memos in a third, held down with a bronze paperweight, and two shelves lined with running trophies.

George snapped her fingers and Nancy looked up. "The light!" George whispered urgently. "Somebody's coming."

Nancy flicked off the flashlight, and the room was plunged into darkness as footsteps echoed in the empty hall. Crouched down, she held her breath as the person passed. A few seconds later she heard the trash can wheels squeal on the linoleum floor as the custodian moved back up the hall.

"All clear," George said. "But hurry. He may be back to pick up the trash in here. What's inside the desk?"

Methodically Nancy opened each desk drawer, searching through the contents with as little disturbance as possible. They contained nothing of interest. "I think we just struck out," she said. "I've looked everywhere."

"Check the wastebasket," George suggested.

Nancy beamed the flashlight down into the

metal basket. Only a few sheets of paper lay at the bottom. She took them out one by one and inspected each carefully. An incomplete attendance sheet, a staff memorandum, some junk mail. Discouraged, she removed the last item—a wadded-up piece of paper—and smoothed it out on the desk.

"George!" she whispered excitedly. "This is it. Look—Sheila Keenan is being blackmailed!"

George moved to the desk and read, while Nancy trained the flashlight's beam on the words. Unlike the crudely handwritten threats Samantha had received, this terse note was computer-printed:

YOU OWE ME ONE, KEENAN
COOPERATE OR YOU'LL REGRET IT

Chapter Ten

"TIME TO GET OUT of here," Nancy said, sliding the note into her pocket.

"Not a minute too soon," George replied, checking the hallway. "The custodian's two doors down. Wait until he goes into the next room and we'll make a run for it."

On George's signal they eased out of the office, sprinted down the hall and out the back door. The rain had stopped completely, and a waning moon shone bleakly through a cloud-streaked sky.

"We may even get an outdoor workout tomorrow," George commented, looking up.

"Maybe," Nancy murmured as they reached the Mustang. She was still puzzling over the note they'd found. "George," she said as she wheeled the car out of the parking lot, "who would have reason to blackmail Sheila Keenan?"

George leaned back in her seat. "Well, it hardly seems like the same people who would send threats to Samantha," she replied. "Lina is Keenan's lead runner. And I can't think of a motive for Matthew. Paul?" She shrugged. "Again, what's the motive? We know they've had arguments about him skipping classes and training, but that kind of criticism just seems to roll off Paul's back. He just laughs at it and does what he pleases."

"The way I see it," Nancy said, negotiating a corner, "there are two reasons for blackmail. Either for personal gain, or to get even with someone."

George whistled softly through her teeth. "And who," she asked, "would have the best reason to get even with Sheila Keenan?" She paused. "The man who lost his job to her—Daniel Abrams."

Nancy sighed. "You're right. I need to talk to him. I'll just have to figure out a logical way to approach him." She pulled up in front of the Faynes' house. "See you tomorrow, George."

The next morning Nancy and George arrived at school well before their first class. On the way they had decided not to say anything to Samantha about the blackmail note to Sheila Keenan or the loose gravel on Mount Fuji.

"She's going to have enough to handle at Paul's party tonight," Nancy said. "There's no point in giving her anything else to worry about."

"There she is," George said, waving at a figure on the front steps.

"Do me a favor," Nancy said. "Stick with her until the first bell. I'm going to talk to Mr. Abrams."

"How are you going to bring up the subject?" George asked. "Excuse me, sir, but I'm trying to identify a blackmailer and I wondered . . ."

Nancy laughed. "Not exactly. Just wish me luck."

"I do," George said as they walked into the building. Nancy gave her a little wave and headed for the coach's office.

Looking through the window in the door of Abrams's office, Nancy saw that the bank of overhead fluorescent lights was on. She rapped sharply on the door and waited. Though she was outwardly composed, inside, Nancy's stomach was churning. She had been awake part of the night, planning and discarding various ways to approach Coach Abrams, and she still hadn't reached a decision. She had learned from experience that sometimes playing it by ear—totally unrehearsed—was the best way to attack a problem. She rapped again and peered through the window, seeing no one in the room. She turned the knob and the door opened. I'll wait for him to come back, she decided.

The room was a typical teacher's office, although quite unlike Sheila Keenan's. Disorderly stacks of papers ringed the floor around the desk, which was covered with what Nancy supposed were the most urgent jobs at hand. A telephone sat in the middle of the mess. One wall held two shelves, loaded with personal trophies and awards, and several framed citations for excellence were tacked above them.

On the other side of the room was a computer and a small printer. With a stealthy look at the door, Nancy moved to the computer and turned it on. It was an older model and seemed to take forever to warm up. Finally Nancy got into the menu. Taking a second glance behind her, she then ordered up the printer fonts, wondering if she would find a match for the typeface on Sheila Keenan's blackmail note. Totally engrossed in viewing the available type styles, she jumped as a sharp voice from behind her spoke.

"I beg your pardon, but what are you doing in here?"

Nancy whirled around. One of the school secretaries was standing at the door, a sheaf of papers in her hand.

"Uh . . . waiting for Mr. Abrams," Nancy mumbled. She reached over and shut off the computer.

"Then you'll have a three-day wait," the secretary said crisply. "Mr. Abrams won't be in until Monday."

"Thanks, I'll come back then," Nancy said, backing out the door. Fortunately, at that moment the first-period bell rang, giving her an excuse to end the conversation. But despite the interrupted visit, she had uncovered one unsettling piece of information. Mr. Abrams's computer was capable of printing out the same font used on the blackmail note.

Cross-country practice that afternoon was outside, and hopes ran high among the team members that the district decision to be handed down Monday would be favorable.

Samantha was still working out at less than full speed, but she had clearly regained much of the flexibility and strength in her ankle. She beamed as they walked to the parking lot after practice. "I loved it," she said to George. "That last run was fantastic. You gave Lina a real run for her money."

"I tried," George said with a grin.

"Can we give you a ride to the party tonight?" Nancy asked Samantha as they reached her car.

"Thanks," Samantha said. "I think I'll drive myself. Then if I want to leave early, I won't spoil your evening."

They watched her pull away and then got into the Mustang.

"How did you make out with Abrams this morning?" George asked on the way back to

River Heights. "We haven't had a chance to talk all day."

"Abrams is off until Monday," Nancy explained. "But I did find out that his computer could have been used for the blackmail note. The only problem is that the font is very common. I checked in the computer lab in my free period this afternoon, and all the machines in there had it."

"So we're no further ahead," George said. "Maybe something will break tonight. Do you know how to get to Paul's?"

"Yes, he gave me a map. He lives in one of those mansions out on the river, about five miles from the school."

"I'm impressed! Do we have to come in jewels and gowns?"

Nancy laughed. "Hardly. Paul said 'definitely casual.'" She veered into the driveway at George's. "Oh, and bring a bathing suit. They have a hot tub. See you later!"

When she reached home, Nancy went to her room and sprawled out on the bed. One disturbing thought after another tumbled through her mind. A part of her eagerly looked forward to Paul's party, but another part kept sending up storm warnings. The one thing she knew was that she couldn't let her feelings for Paul compromise her professionalism.

Finally Nancy got up and started to make

some decisions on what to wear. Slim-fitting black jeans, a scoop-necked jersey and a vintage silk vest made a knock-out combination. A light touch of blush and some lip gloss added a soft glow to her appearance, and she smiled at her reflection in the mirror. "That's better," she said to herself. "It's party night, not doom-and-gloom time."

"Be my navigator?" she asked George when she picked her up later. She passed over the hand-drawn map that Paul had given her.

The drive out to the Johnsons' took them longer than expected. The map led them through the town of Brookline, then onto a curving, narrow road that wound through a rustic, heavily wooded area. Here and there, a rural mailbox served as a marker for an almost hidden private road leading into one of the elegant sprawling estates, tucked away in the dense woods. A rabbit, hypnotized by the headlights, sat frozen on the edge of the ditch that bordered the side of the road until the car passed. The watery light from the slim moon cast an eerie, opalescent glow on the tall pines.

"Spooky," George muttered. "This may be the high-rent district, but it is definitely creepy. We're out in the middle of nowhere."

Nancy wheeled the Mustang around a hairpin curve.

"Nan . . ." George said in a choked voice.

Nancy's breath caught in her throat and her hands tightened on the wheel. A truck, headlights off, lurched from a dark side road, hurtling straight for them.

Chapter Eleven

"Hold on!" Nancy yelled. She gripped the wheel firmly and wrenched it to the right. The truck narrowly missed sideswiping them and disappeared around the curve. Lightly tapping the brakes, Nancy eased the Mustang to a halt at the edge of the drainage ditch and turned off the engine. Then she laid her head down on her arms, which were crossed on the wheel. "Close," she breathed. She rolled down the window and gulped in the fresh night air.

"That idiot!" George cried out angrily. "We could have crashed! And I only got part of the license . . . G twenty-two something."

"Did you get a make on the truck?"

"No, it happened too fast. It was a half-ton pickup, light blue or gray. And it had a camper shell." She looked over at Nancy. "You okay, Nan? That was some great defensive driving."

"Yeah, thanks. I'm okay now." Nancy turned the key in the ignition and slowly pulled back onto the road. "Are we getting close to Paul's?"

George switched on the interior light and studied the map Nancy had given her. "Just up this hill and around to the right. There should be a driveway."

A sturdy-looking mailbox with the name Johnson on it in yellow reflective letters announced the entrance to the estate. Nancy followed the curving driveway through a heavily wooded area for about a quarter of a mile before the house came into view.

"Wow!" George said. "Will you look at that!"

The sprawling ranch-style home of wood and fieldstone was illuminated by ground-level floodlights. Inside the brightly lit front room, they could see people clustered in small groups, some dancing to the heavy beat of a rock band that blasted into the night air. To the right of the house, on a concrete pad, dozens of vehicles were parked side by side and bumper to bumper like eggs in a carton.

Nancy veered toward the parking area and was waved into an empty slot by an enthusiastic teenage boy with a flashlight.

"Last in, first out," George said as she climbed out.

The attendant opened Nancy's door and

grinned in at her. "Leave your keys in the ignition, miss," he said, "in case I have to move your car to get somebody out." He looked over the Mustang appreciatively. "Cool car. Bet it drives like a charm."

"It does," Nancy agreed. "What's your name?"

"Joel Thurber. I live about a mile down the road. Paul hired me to get everybody parked and look after the cars. I'm very careful. I just got my license," he added proudly.

"Okay, Joel, I leave my car in your good hands," Nancy said.

George chuckled as they walked toward the house. "You can bet he's going to find a reason to move your car, just so he can drive it."

"I had the same feeling," Nancy agreed. She turned to George. "Let's not say anything about that truck," she said as they approached the massive oak double doors.

"Do you think it was someone from the party?" George asked.

"Hard to say. But possible."

They stepped into the tiled entry hall and viewed the luxurious living area to their right. Vaulted ceilings added to the spaciousness of the great room at the front of the house. Off to one side, couples were dancing on the parquet floor, and one wall was lined with serving tables, loaded with food. A Persian rug, in a rich blue and maroon pattern, squared off a sitting area, with sofas and easy chairs, and indirect lighting along the walls cast a warm glow over the room. George waved at Amy, who was curled up on one of the sofas, talking to another runner.

"Nancy!"

At the sound of the familiar voice, Nancy turned. Paul was hurrying toward them. He pulled Nancy close in a quick bear hug and then draped an arm around her and George as he shepherded them down the hall and into a game room that was bustling with people.

"I'll give you the grand tour," he said. "You know a lot of these folks."

Nancy smiled at a group of Brookline students who were watching a college football game on a big screen TV that dominated one wall. A pool table at the back of the room was getting some serious use by Matt Lee and another student, and over in a corner, a card game was in progress. Samantha split away from a group to greet them.

"Good news!" she confided, while Paul stopped to speak to one of the card players.

"I could use some," Nancy said. "What?"

"Well, it's not stupendous, but Matt and Lina didn't come together," Samantha said. "They came in separate cars."

"Good! Maybe he's got Lina pegged at last," George muttered quietly to Nancy as Samantha went off in search of some food.

"Maybe," Nancy said thoughtfully.

"Come on outside," Paul said, steering them

toward glass doors that ran the width of the room. He slid one open and they stepped out onto a wide, covered, wooden deck that wrapped around three sides of the building and housed a steaming hot tub.

"I'm impressed," Nancy said, taking a deep breath of the cool night air.

"With the house or the host?" Paul teased.

"Both," she replied, smiling up at him. "And what a magnificent view of the river."

A pale slice of moon shone down on the rapidly moving water, illuminating a private dock about a hundred yards from the house. Subdued landscape lighting turned the wooded area between the house and the river into an enchanted forest.

"What's the building to the left?" George asked.

"That's the boathouse," Paul replied. "We'll go down and take a look later. I want to show you my new toy. Too bad the river's so wild tonight or I'd take it out. But I don't want to chance it."

Back inside, Paul went to greet more arriving guests, and Nancy and George headed for the white-tiled kitchen, where another long table was piled with pizzas, chips, salsa, and sandwich makings.

"My idea of a balanced diet," George said, grinning. She reached for a plate and walked around the table. "I'll fill this up and go find Samantha."

"She was in the great room when we came in. Did you notice Lina anywhere?" Nancy asked quietly, as she followed George.

"Nope, just Matt. He was shooting pool. See you later."

Nancy frowned as she watched George leave the kitchen. Strange that Matthew was not with Lina. Engrossed in her thoughts, she leaned on the counter by the sink and looked out a window toward the river. Some of the partiers had ventured outside and were strolling in the moonlight toward the dock area. Totally absorbed in her thoughts, Nancy froze when she heard angry voices drifting in from outside.

"No, I don't deny it! I called her, too—so what? Where did you get that note, anyway?" The sharp voice belonged to Lina.

"How many of these have you sent her?" Matt's voice was controlled, but angry.

"None of your business! I can't believe this! Samantha whimpers a little and everyone runs to her rescue. First her overprotective Daddy, and now you!"

Retreating footsteps ended the conversation as one of them strode off. Nancy stood stock still, her thoughts racing. So Lina was the one who had written the notes and made the phone calls. But was she also responsible for the acts of sabotage?

Nancy had just decided to head outside and see what else she could find out when she suddenly sensed someone coming up beside her. She turned and was immediately caught in a bear hug.

"Oh, it's you, Paul," she said. "You startled me."

"Startled you? Who else at this party would throw his arms around you?" he asked in mock surprise. "I want names."

"You're a certified nut, Paul Johnson," Nancy replied, laughing. She looked up into his smiling dark eyes and consciously stiffened her resolve to distance herself. It was difficult. He was so charming.

"Ah, compliments will get you everywhere," he replied, winking at her. "What were you thinking about just now?"

"Actually," Nancy replied, "Matt and Lina. I guess they didn't come together."

"Nope. I noticed a bit of a strain between them." Paul took her firmly by the hand and led her out of the kitchen toward the great room. "Now it's time to concentrate on us," he announced.

A slow song was playing as they reached the dance floor, and Paul held her tenderly, his head nestled down into her hair as they swayed in perfect rhythm to the music. The warmth of his body and his breath on her ear turned Nancy's knees to jelly as they moved around the floor. Out of the corner of her eye, she could see Samantha and George watching them. When the music ended, Paul encircled her with his arm and led her to a couch in a quiet corner of the room.

Nancy cleared her throat, trying to shake off the romantic spell. "Samantha says the Beaverton prelims are tomorrow," she said, looking up at Paul.

Paul hooted. "Nancy Drew, you are impossible!" he said. "Here we are, all cozy and warm, good music, perfect atmosphere, and you want to talk about college preadmits."

Nancy grinned sheepishly. "I just wanted to wish you good luck."

"No," Paul said, playfully tapping her nose with his finger, "you really want to know why I'm throwing a party the night before. Why am I not studying? Burning the midnight oil, and all that. Right?"

"Sort of right," Nancy said.

"I'll tell you why," he whispered conspiratorially as he moved closer to her. "It's because the Beaverton preadmits are a piece of cake. No sweat! Old Paul has it all sewn up."

Suddenly the lights in the room flickered and the stereo faltered momentarily. Thunder rumbled overhead in tune with the chorus of groans from inside.

"Not more rain," someone grumbled.

"Come on," Paul said, grabbing Nancy's arm. "I want to show you and George my boat before the sky opens up."

George and Samantha left the group they were

with when Paul wagged a finger in their direction, and the foursome hurried down the stairs from the outside deck and set out across the lawn. A dozen or so kids were still outside, a few by the dock and others on the grassy slope leading back to the house. Some, eager to see Paul's new boat, followed him and the others as they headed for the boathouse.

They crowded inside the small area and admired the sleek, trim craft mounted on a wheeled trailer. Nets and fishing poles were strung from hooks on the walls. A pair of waders sat on a built-in fishing bench, and a creel and spools of fishing line hung from wooden dowels on the far wall.

"When will you take it out, Paul?" Matthew asked, moving in for a closer look.

"Not until spring, now. The river's too wild, and the weather's too unpredictable."

Nancy backed up to join George and Samantha by the door, as others crowded around the boat.

"Sam and I are going to walk down to the dock," George said. "Want to come?"

"We'll be down as soon as Paul finishes showing everyone his new toy," Nancy told George. "Nothing like having a captive audience."

Nancy watched as George and Samantha walked toward the lit wooded area at the riverbank. A few moments later Matthew left the boathouse as well, turning back toward the house.

Others soon followed as dark clouds covered the moon and a sheet of lightning flashed to the south. Thunder rumbled and large drops pelted down from the sky.

Without warning, all the lights went out, leaving the house and yard in darkness. The eerie rushing sound of the river replaced the heavy metal beat of the music, and the hair stood up on the back of Nancy's neck. She stood still, desperately hoping the lights would come back on. Then, suddenly, a scream from the riverbank pierced the air.

Nancy immediately began to run toward the water.

"That's Samantha's voice!" Matthew yelled, appearing out of nowhere and running toward the dock.

Samantha's cries became more frantic.

The beam of a powerful flashlight cut a swath through the darkness as Paul came around from the far side of the boathouse. The light bounced crazily as he ran to the dock, where Nancy stood.

Nancy gasped as the beam from the flashlight shone into the black water and she saw someone struggling to stay afloat in the raging current.

"George is in the river!" Nancy cried out. "Help her—quick!"

Chapter Twelve

GEORGE'S DARK HEAD, illuminated by the flashlight beam, bobbed up and down in the swirling water as she struggled to hold on to a piling at the end of the dock.

Nancy flopped down flat on her stomach beside Samantha, who had found an oar on the dock and was trying to move it into position for George to grab. Paul quickly handed Nancy the flashlight and ran to get a rope, while Matthew slid down the slippery bank, preparing to dive in after George.

"Wait, Matt!" Nancy called to him. "Or you'll both be pulled under. We'll bring her to the edge and you grab her."

Gasping for breath, George kicked against the wild current, grabbed the oar, and clung to it tightly. Nancy and Samantha crouched, then stood, firmly clutching the oar, and backed up along the dock toward the bank, dragging George through the water until she was within reach of Matthew's outstretched arms.

Wrapped in a blanket that someone had rushed down from the house, George was carried back up the lawn and into the warmth of the game room. The lights had come on and the stereo was back in operation.

"What happened?" Nancy whispered to Samantha when they were back inside.

Samantha shot her a cautioning look and silently mouthed, "Later."

George was placed on the leather couch in front of the stone fireplace. Nancy knelt on the rug beside her and rubbed her hands to get the circulation going. George was conscious, but drained of all energy and embarrassed by all the attention.

"I'm okay, guys. Really," she protested weakly. She was still shivering, but the color was starting to come back into her cheeks. "If I could just get some dry clothes . . ."

"Coming right up," Paul said, heading off toward the bedrooms.

"What a scare," Nancy said. "I'm just grateful that you're a strong swimmer. That river's really treacherous."

Paul returned in a few minutes with a pair of jeans and a warm flannel shirt. "Bring her this way," he said to Nancy. "She can change in here." He indicated a guest suite off the hallway. "Have her take a hot shower, too."

Nancy and Samantha helped George into the room and quickly found her a couple of thick towels and a hair dryer.

"Now, what happened out there?" Nancy asked Samantha as George disappeared into the bathroom.

"Well, it wasn't an accident," Samantha replied grimly. "We were walking along the bank—"

"Not on the dock?" Nancy asked.

Samantha shook her head. "No, we were on the bank. George was a little behind me. The power had just gone off, it was pitch-black. I heard a noise, and when I turned around I saw someone behind her. That's when I screamed. The person shoved her into the river and then disappeared into the woods." Samantha shuddered. "I ran back to where she'd been standing, but the current was already taking her toward the dock. That's when I got the oar. The dock was her only hope. If the current had sucked her out into the middle of the river . . ." Samantha's voice faded. "I hate to think what might have happened."

"Could you see who pushed her?"

Samantha shook her head. "It was awfully dark, but I know it was someone about the same height as George. That's really all I saw. It happened so fast I couldn't even tell if it was a man or a woman. But whoever it was knew how to run. The person moved like a deer. But I wasn't going to chase after whoever it was. Getting to George was more important."

Just then George came out of the bathroom dressed in the clothes Paul had given her. "That feels better," she said, sighing. "I didn't think I'd ever be warm again." She looked over at Nancy. "I take it Samantha told you what happened. Any ideas?"

Nancy looked from one girl to the other. "One that I don't particularly like," she said slowly. "You're both about the same height, you both have lean, athletic builds, you both have short dark hair. . . ."

Samantha stared at her. "You think *I* was supposed to be the victim?" she asked.

"I don't know," Nancy replied honestly. "But you'd better be very careful when you leave here. We'll walk you out to your car and follow you home. Just say the word when you want to go."

Some of the guests were leaving when the three of them joined the others in the great room. Through the huge front windows, Nancy could see Joel jockeying cars to the front drive. Then she saw something that made her grab George's arm. "Isn't that it?" she whispered. "The truck?"

Joel climbed out of a vehicle and paused to talk to the driver, who was about to get in. The driver's back was turned toward Nancy, so she couldn't see his face.

George hurried to a better vantage point. "That's it," she said. "G twenty-two is the plate."

Curious, Samantha looked from one girl to another. "What are you gawking at?" she asked.

"That light blue truck," Nancy said. "It almost ran us off the road tonight. Deliberately."

"But—" Samantha stammered. "That's impossible. That truck belongs to . . ."

Before she finished her sentence, the driver swung into the seat and faced Nancy at the window. She was dismayed when she got a good look at his face.

"Matthew?" Nancy said in a troubled voice. "Oh, no."

"That's definitely the truck," George said. "I'll never forget it, coming straight at us."

"Let's go out on the back deck and talk," Nancy said, taking Samantha's arm. "There's too much going on in here."

The three of them walked through the house and outside to the deck. A noisy group had taken over the hot tub, and the girls had to weave a path through clothing and towels that were strewn on the redwood planks. Lina Coleman's voice, loud and abrasive, sounded out as she told a joke to the others.

George walked to the railing and looked out at the river. Drizzling rain still seeped from the dark sky, although the deck itself was sheltered. She stared for a few moments and then turned to join Nancy and Samantha at a wrought-iron table at the opposite end of the deck from the hot tub. "That's a wild river out there," she said somberly.

Nancy nodded, reaching out to touch George's arm. "I hate to think what might have happened," she said softly.

A roar of laughter erupted from the hot tub and broke the serious mood.

"It's been a night full of surprises," Nancy said, turning to Samantha. "George could have been drowned, and we could have been hurt when we were forced off the road. Samantha, it was definitely Matthew's truck. George even got part of the license number."

"It couldn't have been!" Samantha protested. "Matt was here before you arrived. He didn't leave all night." Her voice cracked and she was almost in tears as she defended him. "I know he didn't leave, because . . ."

"Because you were watching him the whole night," Nancy said gently.

Samantha looked up at her and nodded. "I was. It's embarrassing to admit it, but I wanted to see how he acted with Lina."

"But it's a big house, Sam," George argued, "and there were a lot of people milling around. It would have been easy for him to slip out while you were talking to someone."

"But he didn't," Samantha protested.

"How did he act with Lina?" George asked.

"That's the funny part. I didn't see much of her. Maybe they had a fight."

"I think they did," Nancy said, turning to face Samantha. "Listen, Sam. Yesterday I gave Matt the note that was left in your locker. Tonight I overheard his asking Lina about it. He was very angry. She didn't deny writing it, and she stormed off in a huff after he confronted her. And it sounded as though she made the phone calls, too."

"I knew it was her! I was right!" Samantha said triumphantly. She paused and continued in a softer voice. "Maybe I was wrong, too. Maybe Matt does still care about me."

Nancy smiled. "I could almost guarantee it. Tonight when George was pushed in the river, he heard you scream and took off like a rocket. He thought you'd been hurt."

"Are you going to talk to Lina tonight about all this?" George asked.

Nancy shook her head. "I don't want to let her know I'm investigating. It's possible there's more than one person involved. I don't know yet if she's responsible for the other acts of sabotage." She glanced down at her watch.

"Ready to leave?" George asked.

"Almost," Nancy said, staring at the little piles of shoes and shirts and towels on the deck. "Let's hang out here just a little longer." She nodded her head in the direction of the hot tub. The group was disbanding, shivering and squealing in the cool night air as they scrambled for their things and hurried in to the comforting warmth of the house. Lina pulled an oversize sweatshirt over her wet bathing suit and picked up her shoes. "Save me a slice of pepperoni!" she yelled at the boy ahead of her as they went inside.

Nancy rested her chin in her hands and watched until the sliding glass door closed behind them. "I was waiting to see if she'd show any reaction to us." She looked over at George. "Or make any comment about your accident tonight."

"Actually, she could have been aiming for me, when she pushed George in the river, to get back at Matt. . . ." Samantha said. "Since he showed her the note tonight."

"Or she could have been aiming for me," George said, "because until your ankle heals, I'm her main competition."

"Either way," Nancy said, "you both have to be careful." She looked from one to the other. "Ready to go?" They all headed inside, and Nancy searched the house for Paul so she could say good night.

Paul met them just inside the game room. "There you are!" he exclaimed. "I've been looking all over for you. I was about to get up a posse to track you down."

Nancy smiled. "We were just out on the back deck," she explained. "And now we're heading for home. It was a great party, Paul. Thanks."

"Home?" Paul said in mock horror. "We're just getting started!"

"Sorry, but George and I have some serious training to do tomorrow."

"Thanks for the loan of the clothes," George added. "I'll get them back to you on Monday."

"No hurry," Paul said. "I'm just sorry about what happened. That bank is eroding in places. You must have stepped in a weakened spot."

"Must have," George mumbled.

"I'll have Joel bring your cars over," he said, reaching for the pager in his pocket. "Did you all come together?"

Nancy shook her head. "No, Samantha brought her own car. But don't bother Joel," she added. "We'll walk over. After all that good food, we need the exercise."

Samantha and George were already out the front door and headed in the direction of the parking lot. Paul stepped outside and wrapped his arms around Nancy, holding her close as he gave her a warm kiss. "Good night, gorgeous," he murmured in a husky voice.

Nancy steeled her senses as she returned the embrace. Distance yourself, said a voice in her head. "Good night, Paul," she said, looking up into his dark eyes. "I'll see you Monday. And good luck with the test tomorrow."

Breaking away, she hurried after George and Samantha. Joel had already pulled Samantha's sports car up alongside the Mustang.

"This must be a dream job, Joel," George said to him with a grin. "You're allowed to test drive a zillion different cars and get paid for it, too!"

"Yup," the teenager replied. "And I only flubbed once."

"Wrong car to the wrong guest?"

"Not exactly," he hedged. "I can pretty much remember who's driving what. You know, certain people and certain cars go together. Like, the jocks all drive pickups. I had this really cool truck come in—"

"Light blue with a camper shell?" Nancy asked, interrupting him.

"Yeah, and spotlights on the side. How did you know?"

"Just a lucky guess," she said.

"It was right at the beginning of the party and I had a lot of cars coming in at once." He frowned. "The truck was already parked when this girl came out and said she'd forgotten her bathing suit. The truck was in a slot facing the driveway with the keys in it, and she hopped in and pulled out before I could stop her. I found out later that I was right. It wasn't her truck at all." He shrugged. "But she brought it back half an hour later. Gave me a big tip."

"What did she look like?" Nancy asked.

"Tall, blond. Lots of eye makeup."

Chapter Thirteen

"Lina," George said. "Why am I not surprised?"

"I knew Matt wouldn't do that," Samantha said, breathing a sigh of relief. "You could have been killed by that truck!"

Nancy opened the door of the Mustang. "Come on, George," she said. "Samantha, you lead. We'll follow you home."

After seeing Samantha safely park her car in the Materos' garage and go inside, Nancy and George headed for River Heights.

"I still don't get it," George said. "We know Lina left the notes and trashed Samantha's locker, and probably made the phone calls, too. And we know she was driving Matt's truck tonight." She paused.

"And I suppose she could be responsible for

pushing you in the river and for the collapse of the weight bench, but she wasn't around when the lockers fell," Nancy said.

"And she might be the one who sabotaged the course, but I can't see any motive for blackmailing Sheila Keenan."

"That's the sticker," Nancy said. "She's Keenan's top runner now, and they're thick as thieves. George, I really think we're after two people here."

"Lina and . . . ?"

Nancy shook her head. "Maybe Daniel Abrams. I still have to talk to him." She pulled into the Faynes' driveway and George climbed out.

"Shouldn't we be talking to Lina?" George asked again. "Before she thinks up some other little surprise for us?"

"I'd like to," Nancy replied. "But not until I find out who the other person is. They may be working together."

"Got it," George said. "See you tomorrow. We can do ten miles at the park for a change of scenery."

Nancy groaned. "Slave driver," she called out the window as George waved goodbye.

With ten-mile morning runs each day and late afternoon workouts at the local gym, the weekend passed quickly. Early Sunday evening Nancy and George stopped at the Pasta Place for dinner and then headed for their respective homes to deal with assignments that were due the next day.

"Anybody home?" Nancy yelled as she entered the house.

"Hi, Nancy!" Hannah Gruen called down from the top of the stairs. Hannah, the Drews' housekeeper, had been like a mother to Nancy ever since Mrs. Drew died, when Nancy was just three years old.

"There's some leftover casserole in the refrigerator," Hannah said.

"Thanks, but George and I stopped for pasta on the way home," Nancy replied.

Hannah hurried down the stairs carrying her sweater and handbag. "Emily Begley and I are going to the movies," she explained. "Oh, and your dad called. He's staying in the city overnight. I'll see you later."

"Have fun," Nancy replied, giving her a hug on the way out.

The door closed behind Hannah, and Nancy picked up her backpack from the hall and walked through to the kitchen. Tuning the radio to her favorite station, she pulled a notebook and assignment sheet from the bag and sat down to write a character study for English composition. But it was hard to keep her mind on the subject.

Something else was going to happen before the race on Tuesday. She could feel it in her bones.

No case she could remember had frustrated her like this one. There were so many suspects and so many motives. Even the identities of the intended victims were up for grabs. George, Sheila Keenan, Samantha, herself—all had been threatened. How did Daniel Abrams figure into this? And Paul. Was he somehow connected?

Her mind drifted back and forth between the exercise in front of her and the mystery she was trying to solve until the phone gave one sharp ring. The answering machine picked it up immediately, and when the recorded message ended, a man's voice spoke.

"This is Daniel Abrams from Brookline High School . . ."

Nancy leaped off the chair like a shot and grabbed the receiver. Maybe this was the break she was waiting for! She quickly turned off the answering machine and said, "Mr. Abrams, this is Nancy Drew."

"Nancy Drew, private investigator, masquerading as a transfer student?"

Nancy paused. "Yes," she replied. "How did you find out?"

"Ms. Drew, my reputation as a coach and the reputation of the school's athletic department are in jeopardy. I made it my business to find out who you were when you and your friend made such a timely appearance at Brookline and got on the cross-country team."

Go slow, said a voice in Nancy's head. This may be the person you're looking for. "How can I help you, Mr. Abrams?" she asked.

"I believe we can help each other. I'd like to meet with you privately and pool ideas."

"Fine," Nancy replied, with more calm than she felt. "When? And where?"

"I'm in my office now," he said. "Could you come out to the school?"

She hesitated slightly before answering. "I'll be there in thirty minutes."

"Good. Come alone. I'll unlock the side door to the gym."

The dial tone hummed in her ear as she replaced the receiver, only to pick it up again and quickly dial George. The answering machine came on after the fourth ring. Disappointed, Nancy hung up without leaving a message and scooped her homework off the table. So much for English comp. She'd have to take her lumps in class tomorrow.

As she drove to the school, Nancy wrestled with how much information she should give Coach Abrams. Now that he knew she wasn't a legitimate student at Brookline, he could blow the whole case if he talked. And if he was the blackmailer, it would be to his advantage to get rid of her before she had the evidence she needed to expose him.

She pulled up behind a van that was parked close to the darkened school. It must be

Abrams's, she thought as she walked quickly to the side door of the gym. There was no other vehicle in sight. A dim light burned over the entry, and down the long hall a light showed through the window of Coach Abrams's office. She took a deep breath and hurried toward it, rapping briefly at the door before entering.

Coach Abrams whirled around from the computer and waved her to a chair in front of the desk. "Give me a minute to save this." He entered a few more strokes and shut the equipment down. "Thank you for coming," he said brusquely as he moved to the chair behind the cluttered desk.

Nancy nodded and waited for him to continue, unwilling to say anything until he explained why he had called. He stared at her for a long moment with clear and piercing blue eyes.

"As I said on the phone," he began, "I know you're here as an investigator and not a student. I checked the district records. You're already a high school graduate—with honors—and you frequently work on cases with your father—quite successfully, my sources tell me."

In spite of her apprehension, Nancy smiled. "Maybe you should be the investigator," she said. "You seem to be very good at it."

"Not good enough, I'm afraid, although I did do a stint with military intelligence before getting into coaching." Abrams leaned back in the chair and put his arms behind his head. "Ms.

Drew, I'd like to work with you. We're both trying to put an end to the accidents that are plaguing the athletic department, even though I'm no longer officially connected." He paused. "You see, no matter what happens to my career, I don't want to see any more kids get hurt. And that includes you. I understand that you were involved in a couple of situations this past week."

A warning signal went off in Nancy's head. How did he know about those incidents if he wasn't involved himself?

"How do I know?" he asked, echoing her thoughts. "The fellow who came to check the weight-room equipment stopped in to talk. And Mr. Carruthers, the custodian, was very upset with Coach Keenan's accusations. He told me about the lockers falling."

Nancy nodded as she studied him. There was something innately trustworthy about Daniel Abrams. His abrupt manner, she was beginning to see, might not be hostility, but simply a personality so forthright that it had no facade. Either that, or he was a very good actor.

Go with your intuition, said the voice in her head. You'll get nowhere fast if you both hold back. Nancy started to talk. She told him the details about the weight bench collapsing and the bank of lockers falling. "Neither incident was an accident, and Samantha Matero has been receiving threatening phone calls and notes ever since she fell on the track. Her locker's been trashed, and the wipers on her car were broken off," she continued.

"I'm afraid I may have had something to do with that harassment," Mr. Abrams said. "Not directly, of course. You see, I had warned Samantha a number of times about failing to keep to her training schedule. She was often late and sometimes didn't show up at all. Her relationship with Matt Lee was monopolizing her time and hurting her chances to be chosen for a scholarship. I finally had to put her on probation. When she realized I was serious, she broke it off."

"But she didn't tell Matthew why," Nancy murmured.

The coach nodded. "With no apparent reason for the breakup, Matt got angry. That's when Lina Coleman moved in. Lina's a fine athlete but with few ethics. She's an opportunist. She'll scratch her way to the top using any means." He shook his head sadly. "I'd guess she's responsible for the notes and phone calls. She's determined to strip all of Samantha's confidence away, either by scare tactics or dating her boyfriend."

"Well, she went a bit further than scare tactics on Friday night," Nancy said, explaining about being run off the road on the way to Paul's party. She also told him briefly about George being shoved in the river. "I don't know whether Lina was responsible, but if she was, it may mean she's now targeting George as her main competition."

"Possibly." Mr. Abrams paused. "You've been seeing Paul Johnson," he continued, in a tone that was neither approving nor disapproving.

Nancy could feel the color creeping up into her face. "Casually," she replied.

"That's a good way to keep it."

Nancy shifted uncomfortably in her chair. What does he have against Paul? she wondered. Then she shook away the thought and met his stare with unblinking eyes. I shouldn't let myself get sidetracked, she thought. We've talked about everything except the two things in which Daniel Abrams might have played a role.

"Mr. Abrams," she began. "I saw you out walking the track in the rain last week. I wondered why."

"Looking for booby traps," he replied frankly. Then he smiled. "Although I suppose you think I might have been setting some, to make Sheila Keenan look bad." He didn't wait for Nancy to reply. "Well, I didn't find any traps, and I wasn't setting any. I'm not about to put students in danger to settle my own private disputes."

"George and I went out later that afternoon," Nancy said. "We found loose gravel on a mud slick on Mount Fuji." Even as she spoke, a vision of Paul coming in drenched that same afternoon flashed through her mind.

There was a long pause before she continued, and she chose her words carefully. "Did you know," she asked, "that Sheila Keenan is being blackmailed?"

The shocked look on his face gave Nancy her answer. "No, I had no idea," Abrams said, his expression grim. "But I bet I'm a suspect," he stated shrewdly.

"You're the only one I can think of with a motive," Nancy acknowledged. "Keenan's got your job."

Abrams's face flushed with color, and the veins in his forehead stood out. "Ms. Drew," he said, leaning forward, "I believe Sheila Keenan set up the accidents that hurt my runners so she could get my job. Blackmail is too good for her. She should be fired." He held his head in his hands. "I'm sorry, I'm sorry. I shouldn't have said that."

"Do you have any proof?" Nancy asked, a bit startled at the ex-coach's sudden emotion. Her thoughts raced as she considered his words.

"No. But I can tell you this: I'm not blackmailing anyone, and I'm not staging accidents. If Sheila Keenan set those up to get me out of the athletic department, she succeeded. But now the same thing is happening to her. I'm not doing it, but someone is. I don't know if you believe me or not, but I'm grateful that you took time to come out tonight to listen to my side. I knew I wouldn't get a chance tomorrow to talk to you unobserved, but I wanted to let you know that if I can help, I will."

"And you'll keep my identity secret?"

"I will," he promised. "But I'm worried about the race on Tuesday—if our team is permitted to compete. I have a feeling that the accidents aren't over. We'll have to be alert. I'll check the track again on Tuesday." He shrugged into his jacket and stood up. "Come on, I'll walk you to your car."

He turned off the office lights, and together they walked to the side door. Outside, under a clear sky, the air was crisp and fresh.

Nancy climbed into the Mustang and turned the key in the ignition. "Good night," she called to Coach Abrams, and he gave her a quick salute as he bent to unlock the door of his van.

Nancy circled into the drive at the front of the school. Suddenly a vehicle darted out of the shadows ahead of her. Nancy caught only a streak of lights and a squeal of tires as it swerved around a small car also leaving the school grounds, then raced to the main road.

With a surprised gasp, Nancy realized who was driving the speeding car. She stared at the shiny black Cherokee with red and gold markings as it sped away. Outlined behind the wheel were the broad shoulders of Paul Johnson.

Chapter Fourteen

NANCY DID most of the talking on the way to school the next morning, filling George in on her meeting with Coach Abrams and about seeing Paul pull out of the parking lot.

"Who was in the other car?" George asked.

Nancy shrugged. "I didn't get a good look. It was a white compact."

"Keenan drives a white compact. I saw her leaving the other day. Do you think Paul was spying on you or meeting someone?"

"I have no idea. What reason would he have to spy on me?"

"I don't know. Maybe he figured out that you're an investigator and not a student, like Abrams did."

"Maybe," Nancy said, trying to keep her voice

steady. "It shouldn't make any difference to Paul—unless he's guilty of something." She straightened her shoulders. "Well, I'll know soon. First period is history. I'll see if he says anything. He couldn't have missed seeing my car last night."

Nancy lingered in the hall outside the classroom, hoping to catch Paul on the way in. But he didn't show up. And when Sheila Keenan called the roll, she didn't hesitate or even look around when there was no response to "Johnson." Funny, thought Nancy, it's almost as if she expected him not to be here.

The day passed quickly, and Paul never appeared. Tension was high in the afternoon. The district decision on the Brookline team's status was to be announced at two o'clock. A brief assembly was called at two-thirty, and Mr. Lombardi made the announcement. The Brookline team had gotten approval to compete!

A cheer went up from the student body, and a smiling Sheila Keenan hurried to the podium. After thanking everyone for their support and instructing the runners to meet in the gym for practice, she dismissed the assembly. As Nancy left the auditorium, she noticed Daniel Abrams walking slowly back to his office. He must be happy for the students, Nancy thought, but still worried about their safety.

The workout that afternoon was short. In the locker room after practice, Samantha rushed up to Nancy and George, excited about how quickly she was recovering. "I'm getting my endurance back, and my speed," she told Nancy and George. "There are two other schools competing tomorrow, and we've got the best runners. I might even place in the top half."

"Don't count on it," came a voice from behind them. "You're jinxed."

Nancy whirled at the sound of Lina's voice, but the blond girl walked quickly past them and out of the locker room.

"She's so nasty," Samantha sputtered.

"And she doesn't know a thing about team spirit," George added.

"Now that the district has made the decision," Samantha went on, "she doesn't have to be nice to me. She can go back to being her old rotten self."

"Don't worry about her," Nancy replied as she pulled books out of her locker. "I know you'll do well. George will, too."

"Hope so," George said. "Did Paul ever show up today?" she asked Nancy.

Nancy shook her head.

"Maybe he's home, licking his wounds."

"What do you mean?"

"One of the guys who took the Beaverton preadmit on Saturday said Paul was out of there in forty minutes," George explained.

"Forty minutes?" Samantha exclaimed. "That's a two-hour test."

Nancy's forehead wrinkled. "So he either aced it or flunked miserably."

Tuesday was overcast but dry. In the cafeteria excitement was in the air as groups of students discussed the four o'clock race. Lina was the odds-on favorite to win, but George was drawing a lot of support also. And Samantha was getting some well-intentioned sympathy from her non-athlete friends for being at a disadvantage following her accident.

Nancy, George, and Samantha carried their lunches out under a tree, eager to get away from the noisy hubbub of the cafeteria.

"One good thing," Samantha said with a grin. "My dad's in court today. I love his support, but he's nervous as a cat, and he makes me nervous, too. I'm kind of glad he won't be here."

"Paul's out again today, too," Nancy said as they sat down.

"Somebody told me he was sick," Samantha said. "Flu or something." She made a face. "Or maybe he's just sick about Beaverton."

"What do you mean?" Nancy asked.

"He definitely didn't make it. Noah told me this morning."

"Too bad," Nancy murmured. And in the back of her mind she could hear Paul's voice: "No sweat. In the bag. Piece of cake." Obviously that hadn't been true. What could have gone wrong?

Two district buses pulled in at three-thirty, and runners from the other schools took their places out on the field for warm-ups. Sheila Keenan hurried back and forth, clipboard in hand, consulting with the district reps and the coaches of the opposing teams. Nancy observed her carefully from the sidelines. Her normally cool demeanor had disappeared, and it was obvious that she was extremely nervous. Five minutes before race time, she called her athletes together for a brief pep talk. Then the runners lined up for the race. Noisy fans crowded the bleachers, and district administrators clustered near the starting line.

"What's he doing? Checking the course again?" George whispered to Nancy as they watched Coach Abrams across the field adjacent to the starting line.

"Yes. He said he'd walk the course just before the race," Nancy replied. "Just in case there are any new hazards out there."

The last runners moved into place, and a sharp report from the starting gun set off the race. Thirty competitors, ten from each school, ran across the field. Lina and George, wearing the maroon and gold colors of Brookline, were soon out in front, neck and neck, with Nancy holding close behind. When they had crossed the field and entered the wooded part of the course, Nancy glanced back. The distance separating the three lead runners and the pack had lengthened. Samantha, whose strategy was to start slow and finish strong, was somewhere in the middle.

The course, now familiar to Nancy, was in good shape, and the run was invigorating. She grabbed a drink at the first spotter station and raced on, her shoes hitting the ground in a regular rhythm that propelled her along. This is fun! Nancy thought. Whether she was a serious competitor or not, running was a great sport. She could understand why George was so high on it.

George and Lina were well ahead, out of sight now around a bend in the course that approached the pond. Nancy thought about the pleasant hour she'd spent there with Paul. She wished she could figure him out. Shaking away the memory, she decided she couldn't afford to think about that now. Besides, Ned was coming home this weekend. He'd called last night to wish her good luck in the race. She had to admit she'd be glad to see him. Ned was solid. No surprises.

Nancy rounded the bend. Ahead of her, still neck and neck, Lina and George kept pace with each other. Come on, George! Nancy thought. You can beat her!

But in a flash her optimism was destroyed. Nancy's heart skipped a beat as she watched

Lina glance to her right and then deliberately careen into George.

"George!" Nancy screamed out the warning, but it was too late. Lina had pushed George off the track and into the gully.

Chapter Fifteen

NANCY RAN OVER to George, who had rolled down the ravine and landed on her back. As Nancy scrambled down the embankment, George propped herself up and then winced in pain.

Amy Swan shared the lead in the oncoming pack of runners with three students from the other schools. Samantha's red headband pinpointed her in the center of the group as they passed by. She hesitated briefly when she saw George on the ground, but Nancy waved her on.

"Go for it, Samantha!" George yelled at her.

When the last stragglers had passed, Nancy helped George get to her feet.

"It's your knee, isn't it?" Nancy asked, sadly shaking her head.

"Yes, but it's not too bad," George replied,

flexing the knee gingerly. "It's just not up to any more running. And I could have beaten Lina!"

"I saw the whole thing," Nancy said. "She had to go out of her way to bump you."

"Talk about unsportsmanlike conduct!"

Nancy nodded. "It was deliberate."

"At least we got a confession out of it," George said.

"What do you mean?"

"When she crashed into me, she said, 'The river didn't work, but maybe this will!' "

Nancy's eyes flashed with anger. "So it *was* Lina at the river, and she was after you!" With George's arm draped over her shoulder to keep the weight off the injured leg, Nancy guided her through a shortcut back to the school.

The officials, surprised to see the two girls coming from the wooded area, clustered around. Coach Abrams and one of the men from the district hurried to assist George and practically carried her to a bench.

"It's not serious," George protested. "Really. It will be all right after I get some ice on it."

With a distraught look on her face, Sheila Keenan rushed over with a towel and a soft-gel ice pack. "Knees are so unpredictable," she said as she applied the ice. "You never know when they're just going to give out."

George nodded. "Well, my knee didn't give out today until Lina Coleman shoved me down."

Coach Keenan stopped wrapping the leg, frozen in position. Then, slowly, she raised her head. Her eyes narrowed and her mouth turned into a thin line across her face.

"You're lying," she said.

"No, it's true," Nancy said. "I was behind them and saw the whole thing happen. It's not the first time she's tried to hurt George. And she's been threatening Samantha Matero for weeks."

The coach twisted around to face Nancy. "Do you expect me to believe either of you? Of course you're going to back up what Samantha says. It's a perfect setup to get my lead runner disqualified. You'd do anything to make this department look bad!"

"Your department already looks bad," said one of the district officials, moving toward George. "I'd like to hear the whole story, miss. Just what did happen out there? And what about these threats your friend mentioned?"

The woman took notes while George described Lina's action, and Nancy filled in the details about the phone calls and notes in Samantha's locker. A startled Sheila Keenan frowned at first, and then looked embarrassed. Clearly she hadn't known about the threats. Coach Abrams stood beside Nancy, listening to the conversation.

"I want to file a complaint against Lina Coleman," George concluded.

The official nodded. "The district commissioners will want to talk to Lina Coleman, too," she said. She turned to Sheila Keenan. "And there will be a hearing."

"This is ridiculous!" Keenan shouted. "These girls came in here as transfer students, and we've had nothing but trouble since they arrived." She cast a pointed look in the direction of Daniel Abrams. "Someone should investigate who brought them here, and why. Revenge for losing control of Brookline athletics is a strong motive."

Daniel Abrams's face flushed, but he said nothing. Nancy could see him resisting the urge to fight back.

"Exactly what 'trouble' are you talking about?" the official asked. "Are you referring to what these girls have already described, or is there something else?"

Sheila Keenan, suddenly aware that she had said too much, looked away. "Nothing important," she mumbled.

"I think it was important," Nancy volunteered. "I was almost injured twice in the last week." She told about the lockers and the weight bench, while the woman continued to take notes. "There were also two other incidents," Nancy concluded, "but they both happened off campus on Friday night."

Two men, both wearing district official's ribbons, came over as she talked. They listened intently and then huddled with the woman who was taking notes.

Coach Keenan, torn between her anger at Nancy and George, and her need to maintain a cool, professional stance for the benefit of the district people, stood motionless and silent, staring down the field at the finish line.

A touch on the shoulder made Nancy jump. "Paul!" she said. "I didn't see you come up."

"I just sneak around and come out when I feel like it," he said playfully, cocking his head impudently at Sheila Keenan, who glared at him. "Sorry you didn't get to finish the race, Nancy."

Nancy nodded. "I'm sorry George didn't get to finish. She had a great chance at winning."

"Maybe next time," Paul murmured, looking over at George, who was walking very slowly toward the finish line to watch the runners come in. "Let's go down and see them finish," Paul said.

People who had congregated at the starting line started drifting down to the other end of the field, where the course had its finish line. The track, which began and ended on the playing field, provided ideal viewing for spectators.

"We know who's going to be in front," Nancy said grimly as they walked. "It'll be Lina."

There was a collective gasp from the crowd as a runner wearing the maroon and gold colors of Brookline crested the gentle slope that led down to the playing field.

"It's not Lina!" Nancy shouted, rushing to greet the runner. "It's Amy Swan!"

Panting for breath, Amy took the last few strides toward Nancy. "Lina's hurt," she gasped.

"Where is she?" Nancy asked.

"On the last kilometer," Amy said breathlessly. "Take a stretcher. And hurry! She's bleeding badly!"

Chapter Sixteen

THERE WAS A FLURRY of excitement as a student ran to get the stretcher. Sheila Keenan, close to hysterics, grabbed Amy's arm. "What happened?" she demanded.

"I don't know," Amy gasped. "I went up Mount Fuji. She was way ahead of me on the downgrade, and the next thing I knew, she was flat on her face." Amy's voice was shaking. "She must have hit her head. She was bleeding from the forehead. I thought about stopping. . . ." Amy gasped again and looked at the faces around her. "I decided that the fastest way to get help to her was to keep on running."

"Good decision," said one of the men from the district.

Nancy turned and ran toward Mount Fuji, which was hidden from view by a grove of trees at the edge of the playing field. Behind her, she could hear others, also running toward the site of the accident. Ahead, Daniel Abrams had already cleared the field and was entering the woods. Several runners, intent on finishing the race, came streaking toward her in the opposite direction, and Nancy dodged out of their way.

Coach Abrams was crouched on the ground beside Lina, applying a pressure bandage to her head, when Nancy approached. The red blood seeping through the makeshift bandage was a stark contrast to Lina's blond hair and ashen face. Her eyes fluttered open briefly, resting first on the coach and then on Nancy, and she groaned as she regained consciousness.

"Stretcher on this side," Mr. Abrams instructed the students. "Easy now. Keep her level as you go back. Hold that bandage firm." They started toward the school. "And call an ambulance!" he yelled after them. "She'll need X rays. She may have a concussion."

When the last of the runners passed them, he turned to Nancy. "I think the injury looks worse than it is," he said, "but it's bad enough."

Nancy walked to the spot where Lina had fallen. Coach Abrams crouched on the ground and shook his head. "Who would do a thing like this?" he muttered, almost to himself, as he rolled something between his thumb and forefinger. Nancy looked down and saw what he held. It looked like a thin, transparent wire.

Squatting beside him, she said, "It's almost invisible. Is it wire?"

"No," he replied. "Twenty-five-pound test monofilament fishing line." His brow furrowed. "I wonder," he said softly, "if this could have caused Samantha's fall, too."

"Samantha did say there was something strange about her accident," Nancy said thoughtfully. "Almost as if someone had reached out and grabbed her ankle. But wouldn't you have seen the line the day she was injured?"

Coach Abrams sighed. "Keenan was the first one to reach her that day. She could have clipped the line, and no one would have known. The hole was right there to make it look like an accident. No one would be looking for fishing line strung across the track."

Nancy reached for the transparent line. Suddenly a picture of Paul's well-equipped boathouse flashed into her head. She saw the boat, the fishing poles, and the waders—and then the image of reels of fishing line popped into her head. Could Paul have been the one to set up this accident? But why?

"A runner wouldn't have a chance," Coach Abrams said grimly. "She'd never see it. I didn't see it, and I walked the track before the race."

But Nancy barely heard him. Where *was* Paul? She thought he had followed her when she had rushed to find Lina, but she couldn't remember him being in the group that carried Lina back. What if he *was* involved? Did that mean he'd caused Samantha's accident, too?

"Of course," Daniel Abrams continued, "the line could have been set up after the race started."

Nancy stood up and traced the line to where it was tied to a bush.

"The other end is over here on the poplar," Coach Abrams said. "It wouldn't take long to rig up," he continued as they walked back to the school. "A minute. Ninety seconds. Could have been done after I checked the course. I started at the finish line and walked back to the starting line. Someone could have come in after me."

"But why?" Nancy asked.

"To hurt Keenan? To frame me for it? I don't know the answer."

Nancy stopped walking. "Coach," she said. "Paul Johnson wasn't with the spectators when the race started. Do you remember when he arrived?"

"I wasn't paying much attention," Abrams admitted. "He just sort of showed up. Why?"

Nancy hesitated. "Just a hunch. His boathouse is well stocked with fishing line."

"Almost everyone around here has fishing line, Nancy," Abrams said gently. "I'm not a Paul Johnson fan, but owning fishing line is not a reason to suspect someone."

"But there's more than that. Paul showed up at the other two accidents—the lockers and the weight bench—along with Sheila Keenan. And I saw them arguing, twice."

"Sheila Keenan is going to find out what it's like to have a cloud over her kingdom," Coach Abrams said. "For all her fancy Beaverton credentials, she'll have to face the music someday."

Nancy looked up, startled. "You mean Keenan went to Beaverton?"

"She's one of their most highly respected alums," he said. "She proctored the Beaverton preadmits last Saturday."

Nancy stared at him as the truth sank in. "So that's the connection," she said slowly. "I heard through the grapevine that Paul flunked the test. Even though he told me last week that it was in the bag. His inheritance is riding on his admission to the school."

Coach Abrams whistled through his teeth.

"How much influence would Sheila Keenan have on the Beaverton admissions board?" Nancy asked.

"A lot," he replied. "She was their golden-haired girl, an all-school athlete. Some of her records are still unbroken."

"So her recommendation would mean a lot to Paul."

"A lot," he repeated.

Nancy sighed. Suddenly it all seemed clear.

The buses had already left when they reached the school, and only a handful of students were still on the grounds. George was waiting for Nancy and Coach Abrams by the gym door.

"Another 'accident'?" she asked wryly, drawing quotation marks in the air with her fingers.

Nancy nodded and quickly introduced George to Coach Abrams. "Fishing line strung across the track," Nancy explained. "Invisible, but extremely effective. Where's Keenan?"

"Probably in her office," George replied. "She's come totally unglued. She and Paul got into a fight after Lina was loaded into the ambulance. Keenan stormed inside, and Paul marched in after her."

"Time to talk to them," Nancy said, looking from one to the other. "Coming with me?"

They followed her into the school and down the hall to Sheila Keenan's office. Nancy knocked lightly on the door before opening it.

Sheila Keenan was seated behind her desk, toying with a letter opener. Paul stood with his back to the door. "Come in," Keenan said. Her voice and her expression were composed, but her nervous hands betrayed her feelings. "What do you want?"

"Well," Nancy said, looking from the teacher to Paul, who had turned to face them. "There are a couple of things you both need to know. First, Lina's accident was deliberately caused. There was fishing line strung across the route." Sheila Keenan dropped the letter opener on her desk and stiffened.

"And second," Nancy continued, "I'm not a transfer student. I'm a private investigator." There was a flicker of surprise in Keenan's eyes as she glanced quickly at Paul, whose face showed no emotion.

"George is working with me," Nancy continued. "We were hired to find out what was happening in Brookline's athletic department, and we're here with Mr. Lombardi's knowledge."

"I didn't think you were students," Keenan said in a whisper. "Right from the first—"

"Would you tell us what you know about the accidents?" Nancy interrupted.

"Nothing!" Keenan snapped, looking briefly at Paul.

"I find that hard to believe," Nancy said. "I think you hired Paul to set up the first accident, the one that caused Samantha's injury and got Coach Abrams suspended."

Keenan's face drained of color. She opened her mouth to speak and then thought better of it.

"You weren't after Samantha, of course," Nancy continued. "You just wanted an accident that would reflect badly on Abrams, clearing your way to the head coaching job. But you gave Paul a way to ask for something he needed from you. He wanted you to falsify his Beaverton preadmit test."

Nancy looked over to Paul, and her eyes locked with his. For a brief moment she saw a flicker of something like shame in his eyes. Then it was gone. It was as if she were staring at an absolute stranger.

"I think Paul caused the other accidents to try to force you to do what he wanted," Nancy went on. "I think you're being blackmailed."

Sheila Keenan shifted in her seat and avoided looking at Nancy, who continued to speak.

"When you refused, he set up those accidents and threatened to continue until you agreed to his terms. The day that George and I found you on the track in the rain, you weren't looking for your ring. You were looking to see if Paul had set up another booby trap."

Sheila Keenan bit her lower lip and took a deep breath.

"He took your plan to get Daniel Abrams," Nancy continued, "and turned it into his plan to get you. When you flunked him on Saturday's test, he set up today's accident for revenge." Nancy paused and looked from Sheila Keenan to Paul. "Am I right?"

Paul spoke at last. "That's our Nancy Drew . . . gorgeous *and* brainy." He smiled. "You'll understand why I'm not going to say another word without my attorney present. May I go now?"

Charming as always, Nancy thought. How could I have been taken in by him? She turned away without returning his smile. A moment later the door closed behind him.

Sheila Keenan raised her head. "I tried to stop him. I didn't want anyone else to get hurt," she said in a voice that cracked with emotion. "But he wouldn't stop. He thought I'd give in. Paul made a fool out of me! He walked out of that test on Saturday before the first hour was up. All weekend he kept calling me at home. And on Sunday night he followed me here to the school, still badgering me to falsify his score."

George slipped quietly out of the room and returned a few minutes later with Mr. Lombardi.

"Ms. Keenan needs to talk to you privately," Nancy said to him as she led the other two out into the hall.

"Come to my office when you've changed," Daniel Abrams said.

Showered and back in street clothes, Nancy and George waited in Coach Abrams's office until they heard Mr. Lombardi's footsteps.

The principal joined them and perched on the corner of the desk, obviously astounded by the confession he'd just heard. "Of course you'll be reinstated as department head, Dan," he said to Mr. Abrams. "With an apology and a complete explanation to the school board. I've suspended Ms. Keenan without pay until there's a hearing. She's admitted making a deal with Paul Johnson. He wanted grades, and she wanted the head coaching job. But it got out of hand. I have no doubt she'll be fired. And she may face criminal charges as well."

He swiveled to face Nancy and George. "I must admit that at first, I had some concerns about Carlos Matero hiring you. But now I'm grateful to you both for your work on this." He stood up and shook both girls' hands.

"I'm going to call the police," Lombardi said. "They'll want to talk to all of you and issue a warrant for Paul Johnson's arrest."

He stopped at the door and a sad look crossed his face. "Isn't it too bad," he said, "that even the kids who seem to have everything want more?"

Two days later Nancy and George met Samantha after school at the pizza parlor.

"How are things in your life?" Nancy asked as Samantha slid into the booth. "Leg any better?"

"Much better," Samantha said. "If the doctor thinks it's okay, Coach Abrams says I can increase activity another twenty percent next week. Coach is as excited about it as I am." Her eyes twinkled merrily. "I'll be Brookline's lead runner again, and there's a meet in three weeks, with scouts and a chance at a scholarship."

"Great!" George said. "And what about Lina?"

"She's been thrown off the team," Samantha said. "Her head injury was minor. She admitted that she trashed my locker and ripped off my wiper blades. She also claimed responsibility for the notes and the phone calls."

"We had that one figured out," Nancy said between bites of vegetarian pizza. "Umm, this is good! Well, we talked to the police about the two incidents at Paul's party, but without a witness to identify her, they're hard to prove. Even though she admitted to George that she was aiming for her. She was the only serious competition Lina had, since you got hurt."

"Nancy?" Samantha looked up and hesitated. "I just wanted to tell you that I'm sorry about Paul. I mean, I know you really liked him and all. You must be upset."

"Thanks," Nancy replied. "I did like him, but we weren't serious. I guess my pride was hurt more than anything. What's happening with you and Matthew?"

Samantha gave a thumbs-up. "Everything's fine with us," she said. "We're dating in moderation, and I'm keeping to my training schedule."

"Sounds like a happily-ever-after story," Nancy said.

"Almost," Samantha said. "There's just one thing I'd like to change about my life."

Nancy cast a quizzical look in Samantha's direction as the slim brunette scooted out of the booth.

"This," she announced, dragging her backpack off the bench. "Here you two are, free as a breeze, and I'm still hauling around the homework."

George grinned. "You're right," she agreed. "There's one good thing about winding up this case. I might miss running, but I don't miss physics!"

Nancy's next case:

One of the hottest parties of the year has suddenly gone ice cold. Following a major fight with her boyfriend, Tommy Rio, Sharon Krane storms out of the party. And the worst is yet to come. The next day Nancy gets a call from Sharon's father, a River Heights police captain: His daughter has disappeared, and in all likelihood has been kidnapped. Bess's solution: the Extrasensory Convention. Maybe they can get some info from an otherworldly source. Skeptical, Nancy has nothing to lose—except her heart. Master telepath David LeGrand says he feels Sharon's vibrations . . . and Nancy is definitely feeling his. He's all charm and all mystery, and he may hold both Nancy's and Sharon's fates in his hands . . . in *Under His Spell,* Case #116 in The Nancy Drew Files™.

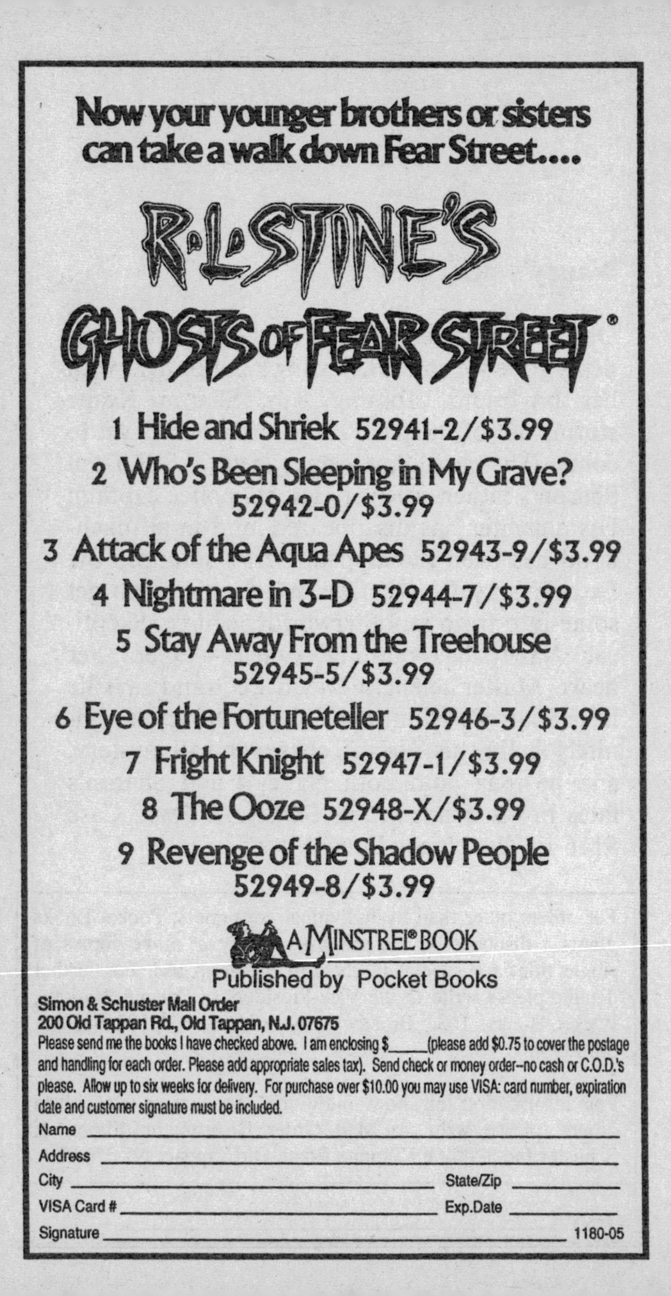
Now your younger brothers or sisters
can take a walk down Fear Street....
R·L·STINE'S
GHOSTS OF FEAR STREET®
1 Hide and Shriek 52941-2/$3.99
2 Who's Been Sleeping in My Grave?
52942-0/$3.99
3 Attack of the Aqua Apes 52943-9/$3.99
4 Nightmare in 3-D 52944-7/$3.99
5 Stay Away From the Treehouse
52945-5/$3.99
6 Eye of the Fortuneteller 52946-3/$3.99
7 Fright Knight 52947-1/$3.99
8 The Ooze 52948-X/$3.99
9 Revenge of the Shadow People
52949-8/$3.99
A MINSTREL® BOOK
Published by Pocket Books
Simon & Schuster Mall Order
200 Old Tappan Rd., Old Tappan, N.J. 07675
Please send me the books I have checked above. I am enclosing $_____(please add $0.75 to cover the postage and handling for each order. Please add appropriate sales tax). Send check or money order--no cash or C.O.D.'s please. Allow up to six weeks for delivery. For purchase over $10.00 you may use VISA: card number, expiration date and customer signature must be included.
Name
Address
City
State/Zip
VISA Card #
Exp.Date
Signature
1180-05